Listen, Layla

Also by Yassmin Abdel-Magied

Yassmin's Story
You Must Be Layla

L-MAGIED

Listen, Layla

PENGUIN BOOKS

PENGUIN BOOKS

UK | USA | Canada | Ireland | Australia
India | New Zealand | South Africa | China

Penguin
Random House
Australia

Penguin Random House Australia is part of the Penguin Random
House group of companies whose addresses can be found at
global.penguinrandomhouse.com.

First published by Penguin Books, an imprint of Penguin Random House
Australia Pty Ltd, in 2021

Cover design by Evi-O studio | Evi O. & Kait Polkinghorne
© Penguin Random House Australia Pty Ltd
Internal design by Midland Typesetters, Australia
Typeset in Sabon Lt by Midland Typesetters, Australia
Printed and bound in Australia by Griffin Press, part of Ovato, an accredited
ISO AS/NZS 14001 Environmental Management Systems printer

 A catalogue record for this
book is available from the
NATIONAL
LIBRARY National Library of Australia
OF AUSTRALIA

ISBN 97 8 17 6089606 5 (Paperback)

Penguin Random House Australia uses papers that are natural and
recyclable products, made from wood grown in sustainable forests.
The logging and manufacture processes are expected to conform to the
environmental regulations of the country of origin.

penguin.com.au

Nobody is free, until everybody is free.
For my family, blood and chosen.
For Sudan, for Ma'ab, for the Revolution.

Note – when Arabic words are written with the Roman alphabet, numerals are used to translate sounds that don't exist in English.

CHAPTER 1

'THE full moon rose over us,' Layla sang, while she carefully joined two pieces of metal together in the broiling, cramped welding bay. The air was hot and humid, not even the whisper of a breeze disturbing the still summer afternoon.

'*Min thaniiiii yatil Wadaaaaa,*' she continued the famous *nasheed* in Arabic, the poem filling in the silence of the workshop. She loved metalwork, and welding while singing was icing on the cake, even if she was totally out of tune. Layla placed the finishing touches on the aluminium bracket, beaming under her welding mask. *Perfecto!*

'And we owe it to show thankfulness,' Layla warbled loudly as she burst out of the welding bay, a hijabi Ned Kelly. She dramatically flung her hands up to the ceiling and started skipping around the work benches, the space transformed into her very own private mosh pit. Soon, the skips became a twirl. *Round and around and around we go!* Layla hummed as she spun, the thick burgundy skirt of her school uniform billowing out around her. For a moment, the fourteen-year-old Australian student was a Sufi whirling dervish from Sudan, the country of her birth. 'Where the –'

A gruff voice interrupted her. 'Layla? Is that you?'

Layla stopped. *Uh oh.*

'Layla, what are you doing?'

It was Mr Gilvarry, her tech teacher. His balding head shone with sweat, his bushy red beard pointing every which way. Mr G was usually quite a jolly man, but right now his face did not look jolly at all.

'Layla, why are you still here? You should really be on your way home.'

'Oh, oops! Sorry, sir.' Layla looked at the clock, which read 3.10 pm. *Janey Mack!* She had completely lost track of time. 'I was just working on the aluminium bracket for our entry into the global Grand Designs Tourismo,' she explained.

Mr Gilvarry raised his eyebrows, sighed, then nodded. 'I figured as much. It's great to see you putting so much effort into the international GDT competition, Layla, but –'

'Yeh, of course, sir, how could I not?' Layla interrupted. 'We're the National Champions now, and we're going to Germany! Not to mention the Special International Invention Tour.'

From the moment she had heard about it, Layla knew going on the first-ever Special International Invention Tour would be her dream come true. The winning student goes on a trip around the world to meet inventors in Paris, Addis Ababa and Beijing! It was Layla's adventuring and invention dreams all in one neat package. Mr Gilvarry was going to select the best student from the GDT team to go, and Layla had become a bit obsessed with trying to win the spot. Needless to say, it was A. BIG. DEAL.

'Yes, Yes, Yes. All of that is very exciting, Layla, don't get me wrong,' Mr Gilvarry replied. 'But it *is* the last day of school for the year, and I'd like to go home now, please. Do you mind packing up so we can both get back to our families?' The tired teacher looked pointedly at the door.

Layla chuckled. 'Yes, yes, yes,' she said, mimicking Gilvarry's voice. 'I'll get everything sorted right now.'

Gilvarry looked relieved. 'Good. I'll wait here. And remember to check your email for the latest competition news, okay?'

Layla nodded, though she wasn't fully paying attention to what Gilvarry was saying. She was pretty excited about the global GDT, but the idea of the SIIT was just *too delicious*! As she got lost in the fantasy of travelling the world, a drop of sweat trickled from her forehead down to her lips. *Mate, it's so hot! Mmm, perfect weather for ice-cream.*

'Ahem, Layla?' Gilvarry cleared his throat impatiently, startling Layla out of her daydream.

'Oh, yup. Sir, yes, sir!'

Walking out of the tech building, across the oval and towards the front gate, Layla reflected on the eventful year she'd had at her new school. Who would have guessed she'd be here? She brushed her hijab back as she made her way through the basketball courts. And to think it all could have gone so horribly wrong after she got suspended.

Layla's train of thought was interrupted as two boys ambushed her from behind, bounding around her and whooping loudly. She'd been hit by the hurricane of her best friends at Mary Maxmillion Grammar School – Ethan and Seb.

'Yeahhhhh, sah-sah-SUMMER!' yelled Seb, his voice breaking slightly as he jumped into the air, landing lithely on his feet before falling into step with Layla. 'Where were you, Laylz? We looked everywhere.' Seb's dark brown hair, floppy as always, covered his eyes. He shook his head to see properly, flicking Layla with drops of sweat.

'Ew!' Layla laughed, pushing Seb good-naturedly away from her.

'Oh, you like it, do you?' Seb teased, then leaned in and whipped his hair back and forth even more vigorously, showering Layla's cream blouse with salty water.

'You're so gross,' sniggered Ethan, the neatest of the group. Even now, with his red hair darkened by the sweat of a Brisbane summer, he was somehow calm, collected and put together.

'Ha, whatever,' Seb retorted, reaching over to muss his friend's carefully styled curls. Ethan yelped as he ducked to get out of the way.

'Still cut, are we?' Layla ribbed cheekily. Seb had been jealous when, a few weeks ago, the school chose the prim and proper Ethan for the cover of next year's MMGS brochure.

Seb scoffed, deflecting the jibe. 'It's not like I care anyway.'

Ethan and Layla glanced at each other. He clearly, definitely cared!

'They shoulda at least had you on the front, right, Laylz? You got way higher marks in class,' Seb said, trying to shift the focus away from himself.

Layla scowled at her floppy-haired friend, whose nose crinkled in confusion. 'What, you think 'cos you got suspended on your first week of school . . .' he started.

'For headbutting the chairman's son,' Layla added.

'Oh yeh, I guess that might make a difference. But still . . .'

Layla rolled her eyes, and Ethan stepped in to save her the explanation. 'Seb, c'mon. As if Chairman Cox is gonna let a Muslim girl with a headscarf and everything be on the front of the school catalogue.'

Seb's eyes widened as it dawned on him. 'Ooooh, yeh, righto. He really doesn't like you, does he?'

Layla smirked as they made their way towards the front gate of the school. 'I don't think he likes any Muslims. Anyway, it's his loss. Who wouldn't want some lush Layla goodness in their lives, you know what I mean?' The teen chuckled to herself as she adjusted the straps of her heavy backpack.

'Forget Cox with a headful of rocks. I was at the workshop, doing some final touches on the GDT idea that I'm working on. Aluminium welding is so tricky, but I'm pretty good now.' She grinned, but before she could continue to wax lyrical about her workshop antics, Ethan and Seb had changed the subject.

'I can't believe it's the end of Year 8,' Ethan sighed, as the three friends meandered through the school campus towards the pick-up area.

There was glitter and confetti all over the concrete path, the aftermath of the various celebrations that had happened during the day. The festive spirit and the green rolling hills of the expansive school grounds made it feel like they were in a magical world instead of a school campus at the centre of Brisbane City.

'I know. It's wild, dude,' Seb replied.

'Oi, you're not listening to me at all!' Layla protested, upset at being ignored. It felt like her friends tuned out anything to do with the GDT.

'Nah, we were, L. It's just you talk about the GDT *all the time*. Like, you're actually obsessed. Didn't anything else happen this year?' Seb asked.

'Um, yeh, it's been a *huge* year,' Layla replied, mildly annoyed her friends weren't as excited about inventions as she was. She started to list all the things that had happened. 'Well, I started at a fancy new school and left the Islamic School of Brisbane behind . . .'

Then Ethan jumped in, poking fun at his friend. 'Seb's voice finally broke,' he teased.

'Ethan declared his love for me,' Seb shot right back, laughing, while Ethan rolled his eyes and scoffed.

'Just because I like boys, doesn't mean I like *you*,' he retorted.

Layla continued, on her own train of thought. 'I helped the Grand Designs Tourismo team win the national competition, discovered my new life mission of becoming a world-class inventor and, most importantly, I have two new best friends!' She beamed at Ethan and Seb, her toothy grin splitting her face in two.

'Aw, you're so mushy sometimes, Laylz,' Seb teased, though his appreciative smile contradicted his words.

He loves it!

Ethan piped up again. 'And you got a nemesis.'

'A neme-who?' Seb wrinkled his nose at Ethan and Layla tilted her head questioningly.

'A nemesis. Like, Layla's sworn enemy, you know?'

'You mean Peter?' Seb asked. He turned to Layla. 'Are you two still enemies? I thought you had to work with him to win the GDT national championship?'

Layla kissed her teeth. It was complicated. 'I dunno. I mean, we're not technically enemies, 'cos I still have to work with him in the team for the international championship, but we're definitely not *friends,* you know?' She sighed deeply. Astaghfirullah. *Why is stuff with the Coxes so difficult?* 'We're not *frenemies,* and *enemiends* doesn't quite have the right ring to it, so I guess . . .'

'Nemesis,' Seb and Ethan said at the same time.

Layla considered it. 'I suppose so. Two new best friends and a nemesis. Not bad for a year's work.' Layla smiled. 'Pretty cool I did it all by myself!'

At that, Ethan shared a look with Seb.

'Anyway, who's picking us up today?' Layla asked, missing her friends' silent jibes.

Since they all lived within cycling distance of each other, their parents had started pooling school pick-ups. Every day, all three friends would pile into the back of one of their family cars, take over the car stereo and loudly sing along to music the whole way home.

Ethan turned to his friends. 'I think it's either you or Seb's,' he said, his even voice almost completely masking the slight undercurrent of sadness in his tone.

'Oh, Eth, your parents still fighting?' Layla asked, her voice soft with concern.

Ethan paused then nodded stiffly. His parents

had recently divorced, and although he had been holding it together so well, Layla knew it was taking its toll on her friend.

'You've gotta remember, it's not your fault, E. It's got nothing to do with you coming out, all right?' Layla squeezed Ethan's shoulder in reassurance.

Seb chimed in. 'Yeh, mate. Listen to Laylz. She's got wisdom,' he hesitated, consulting his phone. 'Or whatever. Anyway, I think it's my mum today.'

'Damn!' Layla exclaimed, and then quickly covered her mouth in embarrassment as Seb widened his eyes in mock offence. Layla backtracked. 'Sorry! Seb, I love your mum, but I really wanted to get an ice-cream from Messina. And you know that's kinda my dad's thing.'

Seb raised his eyebrows, not quite believing Layla's excuse.

'I'm serious, I've been dreaming about ice-cream all arvo.'

Seb rolled his eyes and sighed, wordlessly accepting Layla's explanation. It was a boiling hot day, after all. Then, looking at the throng of people around them, he threw out a challenge. 'Race you to the carpark!' he yelled, taking off without a second glance.

'Ayy!' Layla and Ethan shouted simultaneously, laughing.

Seb had sprinted ahead, his bag half-open, earphones spilling out of his pockets onto the ground, socks falling down to his ankles. The boy was a mess, but rapidly gathering speed. 'Last one to the carpark has to do a dare!' he yelled from afar, turning his head as he ran.

'C'mon, Layla,' said Ethan, breaking into a jog.

'It's too hot for this,' she grumbled, but she too picked up the pace.

Layla and Ethan soon caught up to Seb and the three friends ran after and beside each other, weaving in and out of kids and parents, jumping over flowerbeds and startling a few cute puppies along the way. Layla felt like she was gliding on air. There was a tailwind behind her, pushing her onwards and upwards, and her hijab felt like a cape, marking her out as a superhero. She was ready to take on the world and all it had to offer. Was she Ms Marvel? Carmen Sandiego? The Queen of Sheba?

None of those.

As she sidestepped a toddler and vaulted over the carpark fence, her skirt unfurled and snapped back like a handheld fan over the metal divider. She wasn't a copy of another hero. She was her own. *I am Layla Kareem Abdel-Hafiz Hussein, the greatest Sudanese Australian inventor the world has ever seen. And if they don't know my name yet, they soon will.* Inshallah!

CHAPTER 2

THE trio sat on the curb, playing on their phones, when a black Lexus rolled up. Seb's mother sat upright in the driver's seat.

'Finally,' gasped Seb, jumping to his feet and slinging his bag onto his back.

'Do you think I could convince your mum to take us to Messina?' Layla asked Seb hopefully, as they stood on the asphalt.

Seb snorted. 'You're really trying it, huh?'

'What?' Layla replied, grinning. 'I've gotta give it a go. I've *seriously* been thinking about it all arvo.'

Ethan shook his head, amused. 'You know how strict his mum is.'

Layla wiggled her eyebrows up and down. She loved a challenge!

'Hi, aunty,' called Layla, brightly, as she slid into the back seat with Ethan, clicking her seatbelt in.

'Hello, *mis amores*,' called Seb's mum from the front seat. She reached over to turn the radio down, perfectly manicured nails painted a classic white.

Layla thought Seb's mother was so *sophisticated*. 'You look so nice today, aunty!' she piped up.

The Colombian matriach wore a sharp teal suit, which contrasted strikingly with her olive skin and black hair, cut in a short, neat bob. Not a single strand was out of place. *Mashallah!*

'Thank you, Layla,' she replied without turning around, stroking her son's face gently. 'If only Sebastian would learn from me, mmm?' Seb moved his head out of his mother's reach, moodily.

Layla looked over at Ethan, a cheeky grin painted across her face.

'Don't do it!' Ethan whispered, on the verge of laughter. 'Don't! I can't handle it. Seriously!'

Layla's chin quivered with mischief, and then she raised her voice.

'So, aunty, any chance we could get some Messina on the way home?' Layla held her breath.

Silence.

The quiet stretched, filling the car with ice, and not the kind that tasted of salted caramel. Ethan arched an eyebrow at Layla. 'You never listen!' he seemed to say.

Lol . . . Maybe Ethan was right after all.

Layla jumped out of the car at the front of the shopping centre, where her father had asked for her to be dropped off. The hijabi's long maroon skirt stuck to the backs of her thighs as she emerged out of the cool aircon into the stinking summer heat.

'Bye, guys,' she called, waving at her friends.

'See you soon, L,' Seb replied through the open window. Both boys waved as the Lexus smoothly pulled away, the blacked-out glass pane reflecting Layla's goodbye.

Layla found Kareem with her brother, Ozzie, at the trolley collection bay on the lowest level of the multistorey carpark. By the time she got to them, her blouse was doused in sweat. How was Brisbane heat so intense?

'Baba, Ozzie, what are you doing down here?'

Ozzie stood forlornly, a fluorescent orange vest over his baggy Tupac top. Kareem, slightly shorter than his eldest son now, stood proudly next to him, hand on the teenager's slumped shoulder. Baba was in the outfit he always wore – grey slacks, comfortable old-man sandals and a checked button-down shirt.

'Layla, your brother is the newest employee of the Trolley Collecting Enterprise.' Kareem smiled, looking at Ozzie.

'Oh, *mabrook*, Oz! You got a job. Finally!'

Ozzie shot his younger sister a deadly glare. 'Shut up, sis.'

'C'mon,' Layla said, hurt at being rebuffed. 'You've been job hunting for ages.' Layla eyed her brother. 'Why aren't you happy, Ozzie? This is a good thing, right?'

He frowned. 'I am happy,' he muttered, the words not matching his demeanour at all.

Kareem stepped in. 'My friend, you know Uncle Adel, is now running the trolley collection company here at the shopping centre. Ozzie did an interview today, and now has a job!' Baba turned to his son. 'Ozzie thinks he is better than this, but we all have to start somewhere, right? Whatever others might think.'

Layla paused, remembering the big heated discussion that the family had had at dinner a few days ago. 'Wait a minute, Baba. Was this the job that Mama didn't want Ozzie to do?' Layla's jaw dropped at the brewing scandal. 'Does she know about this?'

Ozzie had been searching all year for work with absolutely no luck. Some bosses said he didn't 'fit the look' of the company, and others didn't bother responding to his applications at all. He'd even been rejected from places that had signs on the front saying 'STAFF NEEDED'. Fadia, their mother, was not a fan of Ozzie taking any old job he could find, thinking that some positions were a waste of his potential. But it looked like Ozzie had followed his dad's advice instead: to take whatever work he could get. Whether he liked it or not was a different question.

Before Kareem could reply, they were interrupted by the excited squeals of Layla's younger twin brothers bursting out of the shopping centre doors.

'Layla! You're here!'

'Oh, you're here too!' Layla said, greeting her younger brothers with an ear-splitting grin and a kiss on each of their foreheads. Sami and Yousif nodded simultaneously. 'Where have you been?' Layla asked.

'We were at the library.'

'Baba said we can get some ice-cream if we stayed quiet until five o'clock.'

'It was so hard!'

'Can we get ice-cream now?'

'Yeh, and then can we go to the park and play, pleeeeeeeease?'

The twins, beyond excited at the prospect of two months of summer holidays after their first year of school, could barely contain their energy.

'Basketball?' suggested Sami, jumping up and down on the spot, clutching at Layla's backpack and drumming his little hands on her arms.

Yousif, on the other side of her nodded, and chimed in. 'What about, what about, we go for a bike ride?' He was offering his favourite activity as an alternative to the ball game where the twins both knew they would be thoroughly beaten by Layla. Despite her short stature and stocky figure, Layla was quick on her feet. *Call me LeBron's little sister!*

Sami smiled widely, showing off his missing front teeth in an effort to charm his older sister.

Layla chuckled, enjoying her brothers' attention. 'Okay. Ice-cream time, then home?' she suggested, looking at her dad to confirm. With Kareem's smile of permission, the ice-cream-keen teen took her younger brothers' hands and led them back into the shopping centre for their promised treat, their father trailing a few steps behind.

'Isn't Ozzie coming with us?' Sami asked. 'Where is he going?'

'Ozzie's got a job now, so he's got to get to work,' Layla explained. 'But he will drive us in that special trolley car later, *tamam*? That'll be fun, *mushkida*?' Layla ruffled Sami's tight curly hair as they walked through the shopping centre. 'So, tell me about your last day of school,' she said.

The twins regaled their older sister with their afternoon antics, not quite finishing any thoughts, but ending each other's sentences with gusto and enthusiasm. The sight of the ice-cream shop abruptly brought the catch-up to an end as the attention of all three kids was stolen by the glorious selection of frozen goodness in front of them. The boys leaned on the cool, curved glass of the display cabinet.

'Yousif, you're drooling on the glass!' Layla admonished lightly, hurriedly wiping clean the saliva snaking its way across the display. Sami giggled at his brother as they put their heads together to discuss ice-cream flavour preferences in hushed, serious tones.

Kareem stood a little way back, a muted smile on his face. As she placed the ice-cream order, Layla grinned. *It feels like it's going to be a good summer!*

Just as they were about to leave the shop and head home, Layla bumped into Penny, a girl from the GDT team, also getting her creamy dessert fix.

'Hey, gurl,' Layla said. Even though they weren't super close friends, Layla liked Penny. She was definitely the nicest in the GDT group. 'See you around sometime, yeh?'

Penny tilted her head curiously. 'You mean tomorrow, right?'

'What?' Layla paused in the doorway of the shop. 'What's tomorrow?'

Penny shook her head with disbelief. 'Layla, you need to check your emails more regularly.

Mr Gilvarry is announcing the winner of the Special International Invention Tour spot tomorrow!'

Penny laughed at the look on Layla's face as she stood frozen in place, melted mint choc-chip ice-cream trickling down her arm. The Special International Invention Tour winner was going to be announced tomorrow?! On the first day of holidays? Why hadn't Mr Gilvarry said anything about it when she saw him this afternoon?

'What?' Layla was shocked. 'I thought he was announcing it next week?'

Penny shrugged. 'Yeh, I dunno. His email said something about going on holiday, and he wants to be the one to deliver the news. So . . . guess it's tomorrow.'

A bolt of adrenalin ran up Layla's spine.

Oh, I totally forgot to check my email! Oh, ya Allah, *help me win!*

'Layla? Anyway –' Penny's mum called out in Cantonese, interrupting. Penny turned. 'I gotta go. Tomorrow?'

'Yeh, of course. See you tomorrow.'

Janey Mack! Thank goodness she bumped into Penny. That was a close call. She raised her face up to the sky. *Thanks for that one,* Allah.

CHAPTER 3

THE next morning, Layla's eyes snapped open, and she grinned to herself, wriggling in her pyjama *jalabeeya* underneath the light bedcover. 'Today is the day Gilvarry announces the winner of the touuuurrrrr!' she sung to herself, slightly out of tune as usual.

Leaping downstairs, after an exceptionally quick teeth-brushing and two *rak3aat* for *fajr* morning prayers, Layla skipped into the kitchen. This was the heart of the Hussein family household, but right now it was quieter than usual. Ozzie had left the house early to go to work.

The only other person up was her father, bustling about to the background drone of Arabic news on TV. Layla heard the journalists talking about Sudan, but dismissed it, her focus on Baba.

'*Sabah alkhair*, Baba,' Layla said brightly, as she slid onto one of the wooden stools at the kitchen bench.

Kareem was standing at the sink, washing dishes, the sleeves of his shirt folded up to avoid the suds. '*Sabah alnoor*, ya Layla. Someone's up bright and early.'

'Yeh, I woke up so early. Mr Gilvarry is announcing the winner of the Special International Invention Tour today!' Layla bounced up and down on her stool. 'I want to go see Dina first though, *mumkin*?'

Kareem turned to look at his daughter. Layla's curly afro was coming out of its hair ties and standing on end. Her *jalabeeya* was crumpled and starting to tear slightly, and her dark brown skin was ashy from lack of moisturisation. It would have been a sorry sight if it weren't for the huge grin on Layla's face.

'That's the tour you have spent all year working towards? Okay, *yallah*, *khair Inshallah*. But let's wait until everyone else is up before you see Dina, *tamam*? Now, why don't you go upstairs, get dressed properly and then come back down for breakfast? *Bayd tashtoosh.*'

Tashtoosh! The teenager licked her lips and jumped off the chair, running back up to the bathroom. She didn't know what her dad did to make eggs so delish, but they were her absolute favourite. *Om nom nom!* It was like they were fried in *heaven*.

That afternoon, Layla sat on the swing at the park alongside Dina. Ethan and Seb were playing basketball nearby. Layla's thick brows were furrowed as she pumped her legs up and down, swinging herself higher and higher.

'How do you feel about this year?' Layla musingly asked her best friend, as her swinging slowed down. Dina was Layla's OG bestie, whom she had known since they were kids. They had gone through primary school together, and Dina had remained at the same school after Layla received the scholarship to MMGS. Layla had been worried that the new girl at ISB, Bushra, would replace her in Dina's heart, but fortunately Layla and Dina's friendship had lasted their school separation.

'What do you mean?' Dina asked.

The pair had been swinging in silence for a few minutes now, watching Ethan and Seb tussle with the orange rubber ball. The boys were both pretty hopeless at basketball, but what they lacked in skill, they made up for in enthusiasm. It was quite entertaining to watch.

'Oh, I dunno. I was just thinking about how so much has happened,' Layla reflected. 'I mean, to be honest, Dina, I . . . I don't think I'm an adventurer any more.'

'Really?'

Layla took a deep breath in a moment of contemplation. 'Yeh, I mean I still love climbing trees and bejewelling, but being at MMGS made those things feel really . . . uncool.'

Dina scoffed. 'Layla, you're the coolest person I know.'

Layla abruptly stopped swinging and frowned at her friend, her expression incredulous. Then they both burst out laughing simultaneously.

'I've never been cool, D, lol!'

'You're cool to me.'

'Aw, stop it!'

'For real though . . .' continued Dina.

'I know, I know. But I'm not cool, cool, you know? Like, I think I'm cool to myself, but in the entire ecosystem of coolness, I'm not a great white shark. I'm more like . . . a wombat.'

'A wombat?'

'Yeh. Low to the ground, staunch, but no one messes with a wombat.'

Dina started laughing again. 'Layla, what are you on about? You don't look anything like a wombat to me.'

'Okay, okay, whatever. Enough about animals. All I know is that the GDT fully changed my life and showed me a whole new world. I really, really hope I get picked for the SIIT, Dina, *Inshallah*. It would be so wonderful to travel the world, to meet all those brilliant people!'

Dina's nose twitched and her eyeline shifted up to the sky.

'Dina?' Layla asked, wondering what her bestie was thinking.

Her Pakistani friend glanced down, a strand of hair slipping out from underneath her loosely tied scarf. She then met Layla's eyes. 'You're lucky, Layla. You've always had big dreams, and your parents support them, no matter how wild. But my dad is already talking to me about how important it is to get married . . . and you know my sister didn't even go to university. So –'

'So what?' Layla interrupted. 'You're *so* smart, D. You'll get a scholarship to go to university for sure, and then you'll be on your way to becoming a big-shot lawyer, like you always dreamed, *Inshallah*. You'll be locking up war criminals in no time, right?'

'The only thing Dad said he'd let me be is a doctor. Either that or get married.'

'D, you've got to be joking. That's wild. We just finished Year 8. You can't be talking about getting married. Also, you hate biology!'

'It's never too early to start "talking", Dad said.'

'What does your mum think?'

Dina looked mournful. 'She hasn't said much.'

An understanding silence fell between them. Dina's mum had been quite ill for most of this year, so her older sister had started helping out a lot more around the house. Layla felt sad, realising that her friend was facing a very different future to herself.

Only a year ago we were planning to adventure through the world together. Now, well, Allahu a3lam.

'Janey Mack, D. What are we gonna do? Maybe I can invent a time machine to fix it.' She tried to joke, but it fell flat.

Dina shrugged, seemingly resigned. 'Dunno, L. Go to the mosque more?'

Layla scoffed. 'There is literally not a single cute guy at the mosque, D. We have known them all since we were kids.'

Dina chuckled. 'I'm just happy hanging with the Fantabulous Four for now.'

Layla's face instantly broke into a smile. '*Finally*, someone calls us the Fantabulous Four! I told you I come up with great names.'

Dina snickered under her breath. 'It's all right.'

Layla reached over to grab her friend's hand. 'We'll figure something out,' she said soothingly.

D nodded before throwing the question back to Layla. 'What about you?'

Layla hummed as she started swinging again, mulling on Dina's question.

'I just hope I get picked for the Special International Invention Tour.'

'Oh yeh, when's the announcement?'

'Later this afternoon.' Layla's eyes widened, and then she looked at her watch.

'Like, now!'

Ya-nahr-aswad! She was going to be late!

Scrambling off the swing, Layla bolted down the street back to her house. How would she ever be a great inventor if she couldn't even make it to a meeting on time?

CHAPTER 4

LAYLA caught the bus. Just. *Phew!* She settled into a seat towards the back, puffing from the run to the stop. *Lucky Dina reminded me,* Alhamdulilah! Looking out the window as the bus hit the highway, she started daydreaming about what it could be like on the Special International Invention Tour.

Imagine going to Addis . . . what will it be like?

'Miss? Excuse me, miss?' The young man sitting in the window seat next to her startled Layla out of her reverie.

'Yuh?' she asked cautiously, her mouth suddenly dry.

What did this stranger want? The hairs at the back of her neck prickled. Was he going to yell at her about being a Muslim terrorist or something? Layla braced herself for the verbal barrage.

'Sorry, I just need to get out at this stop,' the guy said.

'Oh, haha, of course.' Layla unclenched her jaw and breathed a sigh of relief as she jumped up and out of the way, letting the man pass.

It's okay, it's okay, she soothed herself. Layla slowed her breathing down, inhaling deeply, calming her nerves. *Only a few more stops until school, you've got this, you have just as much right to be on this bus as anyone else.* Layla was always thrown by how seemingly small moments like that could turn her whole day upside down. *But today is not that day!* Today was all about the SIIT. Layla focused on her breathing, praying for the bus ride to end.

The school stop finally arrived.

Hitching her backpack on her back, Layla walked through the quiet school grounds to the tech building. She remembered when Baba drove her and her brothers to these grounds for the first time last year. It had seemed too good to be true. Who would have guessed she would be a prize-winning student at MMGS only a few months later? *Subhanallah*.

'Layla, you made it,' a familiar voice called from behind her.

Layla turned around and smiled. 'Hey, Penny. Yeh, I did. Thank goodness I bumped into you yesterday, honestly. I had definitely not checked my email.'

Penny smirked, though not unkindly. She was in the grade above, and they had become friends over the year while working on the GDT project. Matt and Tyler, the other two members of the team, joined Penny and Layla at the front door of the tech building, waiting for either Mr Gilvarry or Peter, who both had keys.

'You ladies ready for the announcement?' said Matt.

Penny and Layla exchanged glances.

'Yeh,' said Layla, working hard to mask her nervousness. 'Peter will probably get it, won't he?'

Tyler chuckled. 'Probably. But we know you want it, Layla. You've been busting hard for it all year.'

Layla looked down at the concrete ground bashfully. Her teammates had often seen her working late, trying different things out in the workshop, sketching and building and sketching and building, all in an effort to be a better inventor (and yes, also win the SIIT).

'Well, you know. Can't let Peter have it too easy now, can we?'

Suddenly the door of the tech building screeched open and a tall, gangly boy with a shock of platinum hair stood on the other side – Peter.

'Did I hear my name?' he said, looking at each and every one of his teammates dead in the eye, but no one responded.

'Whatever. Get inside already,' Peter snapped, brushing blond hair out of his eyes.

Meekly, the team members filed up the stairs and walked along the long hallway towards the main workshop, their footsteps echoing in the concrete passage.

Layla always felt like she was coming home when she entered the workshop. Rays of after-noon sunlight streamed through the glass roof. The familiar scent of varnish, turpentine and metal hung in the air. The room smelled of potential, possibility and hope. Here, anything could happen. Including a concert for one in the welding bay.

Mr Gilvarry was sitting inside his office in the back of the workshop area, but the teacher came out when he heard the GDT students come in.

'Okay, team! How are we doing? We feeling *ready* to take on the *world*?!'

Mr Gilvarry was a masterclass in enthusiasm.

'Yes, Gilvarry, we are,' Peter said, characteristically terse. 'All right, everyone, grab a spot.' As the team took their seats around a workbench, Peter kept talking. 'Layla, as secretary you're taking minutes, right?'

Layla barely had time to nod before he continued.

'Gilvarry and I have been looking at plans for the global competition in February, and it's pretty clear we've got a long way to go before we're ready.'

'Why?' Penny asked. 'I thought it was all fine?'

'It was fine, but remember the judges recommended we do something more innovative if we want a shot at winning the international GDT. None of our current ideas hit the mark. We need to level up.'

'Can we do everything we need to in time?' Layla asked. Not only did they have to work on the actual invention, but there was the matter of organising all the travel stuff for their trip to Germany. It was going to be tight.

'It's not about whether we can, Layla. We must. So, Gilvarry and I have agreed on a new system. Instead of once a week, we meet at least three times a week, to make sure we get everything done. If you miss more than three meetings in a row, you're off the team. I'll find someone else to replace you.'

'What?!' Everyone burst out simultaneously.

'Pete, isn't that a bit harsh?' Tyler asked, trying to get their leader to loosen up a little bit.

'Do I look like I'm joking?' he retorted, waiting for a response.

Tyler fell silent. After a moment, they all shook their heads.

'I know you think I'm being too hard, but trust me. We need to come up with something that works, something brilliant that will blow everyone in Germany away. We want to win, don't we?'

Silence.

'Don't we?'

The replies came hurriedly, again all at once.

'Yeh!'

'Oh yeah, of course.'

'Damn *straight*!'

'Yes, sir!'

'A hundred and ten percent from all of you for the next two months, okay?' Peter said.

They all nodded dutifully.

'Especially you, Layla.' Peter made sure to get a barb in.

Layla kissed her teeth at the uncalled for comment.

'Fine. Now, let's get to work.' Peter turned to Layla. 'Got those brainstorming notes from last meeting?'

Layla frowned slightly, wondering why the SIIT winner hadn't been announced yet. Maybe Gilvarry was trying to build the drama. But it was already so dramatic!

'Layla?' Peter prompted.

Layla nodded, pulling out large sheets of paper from her backpack. She unfolded the butcher's paper they'd worked on, covered in colourful squiggles and arrows and brainstorm bubbles. *Electric scooter* was circled about ten times, with *medical support* also highlighted. They had been searching for different uses for their current robot design, and how to make it super, extra, ultra impressive, so that it had a real shot of winning the international competition.

'Some of these ideas are pretty cool, but we would have to start from scratch.' Layla pointed at *incredible ice-cream maker*. The page was also full of Layla's notes and drawings from her many lunchtime and after school sessions alone in the workshop. 'We need to use our imaginations a little more, right, Peter?'

Tyler and Matt nodded, but there was no response from the team leader. Layla, registering the absence, looked up from the table. 'Wait. Where's Peter?'

'I'm here,' he said, walking back to the workbench. 'I just wanted us to remember where we are starting.' Peter had retrieved the robot from storage and placed it on the counter, right next to the pile of brainstorming pages.

It was pretty incredible. The invention was a humanoid robot, the size of a small child, with an iPad screen instead of a head. The body and legs of the robot were held up by a neat skeleton of Meccano pieces draped in opaque carbon fibre the colour of toffee to represent the skin. Instead of feet, there were wheels: thick, fat wheels with deep treads, helping it to traverse all sorts of terrain. And in place of hands were Layla's gummy bear actuators, the invention she came up with at the beginning of the year. The colourful, edible creation had helped get this robot over the line at the state competition and onto the podium.

Layla still felt so proud every time she saw those hands. *And I made them all by myself!* That made her extra proud. She always felt like it was best to depend on *yourself* to get things done.

As the team continued to chat and brainstorm around her, Layla settled onto her stool, cleared her mind and focused on taking notes. It was GDT time. They were in it to win it, *Inshallah*. Especially her.

As the meeting drew to a close, a slight tension hung in the air. Everyone knew the announcement from Gilvarry would happen any moment now. Right on cue, their tech teacher walked out of his office and stood at the head of the workbench.

'Now,' he declared, bushy moustache bristling. 'I know you've all been working towards this moment. It isn't every day that I get to select someone for something as prestigious as the inaugural Special International Invention Tour. It's not an easy decision, which is why I asked you all to make a submission: either an essay or item that would convince me you are the best person to represent Australia on the tour.'

Layla glanced around at her teammates. Penny's eyes shone bright and hopeful. Matt and Tyler were trying to be cool, but they obviously cared. Peter looked . . . frightened? *Weird.*

'Obviously, your marks in every subject this year are also taken into account. So, if you have been focusing on tech at the expense of everything else – like Matt – then, I'm sorry, you won't be going on the tour.'

Matt's shoulders slumped.

'Tyler, same for you, I'm afraid. Your English grades didn't cut the mustard. This showed up in your essay, unfortunately. Maybe next time build something instead. You're better with your hands.'

Ouch, Mr G, that was cold!

Gilvarry studied the remaining three – Penny, Peter and Layla.

'Penny, you've had an exceptional year, grades wise. The essay you submitted was also very well written, but it didn't convince me that you would get anything unique out of this exceptionally exciting opportunity. So, you'll be sitting this one out.'

Penny's expression sank slightly, but she acknowledged Gilvarry's compliment with a graceful bow of her head. Mashallah, *she is one classy lady.*

Before he continued, Gilvarry looked around at them. 'Remember, you all go to the GDT in Germany, okay? The SIIT is special, yes, but you are *all* winners.'

'Aw, c'mon, Gilvarry. Don't keep us waiting,' Peter urged.

Peter had a hungry, desperate glint in his eyes. Layla felt a *tiny* bit sorry for Peter. She knew that his father, the chairman of the school (who also had a personal problem with Layla), put a lot of pressure on him. *But that's not really my problem. Plus, it's not an excuse for being so mean all the time, like he is.*

'As you wish, Peter. Now, your submission of an air-quality sensor was pretty handy, I will give you that. There are lots of places around the world that have air quality issues . . .' Gilvarry paused for effect.

Layla's heart was in her throat.

Was this it?

CHAPTER 5

LAYLA skipped up the path to her house, humming loudly. The Hussein family lived in a modest brick home. Layla thought it looked like a house designed by a kid; it had a long and flat rectangular front with a few big windows, a brown double garage on the right-hand side and a neat, dark red triangle roof that was turning a bit brown in places. Green bushes lined the red-brick path up to the welcome mat at the foot of the front door. Layla opened the screen door first, holding it ajar with one hand. She then turned the house key in the front door, unlocking the dead lock with a thud and pushed against the wood with her shoulder.

'Hellooooo, I'm home!' she announced, bounding in with excitement. 'And guess who got selected for the Special International Invention Tour?'

Layla couldn't believe it! All her hard work throughout the year had paid off. Mr Gilvarry also appreciated that she had gone the extra mile by building something, writing an essay *and* getting good grades. Shutdown Mode had really worked.

I channelled the jamel *all the way to Germany and beyond!*

As she skipped down the corridor, it slowly dawned on Layla that her voice was echoing around the house with no reply. Something was off. There was almost no sound at all, save for some low murmurs coming from her mother and the TV.

Hmm, weird.

By this time of day, the house usually resembled a chaotic Sudanese *souq*, with loud music, good-natured yelling and lots of sumptuous food smells. Today, the house was more morgue than marketplace.

Layla slowly walked into the main living area, taking her hijab off and setting her braids free. The twins sat forlornly around the dinner table, Baba stirred a pot in the kitchen and Fadia whispered urgently on the phone, pacing up and down in front of the TV, twirling the end of her long braid around her index finger. Something was clearly wrong. Layla hadn't seen the house like this, since, well, ever.

'Hello!? Anybody?'

When no one responded, Layla tried a different tack. 'What, did someone die or something?' she joked loudly, hoping her comment might break the ice.

She couldn't have said anything worse. Mama shot her a warning glare, laced with a vein of something else – was that fear? – while the twins squirmed in their seats, unusually silent. Kareem paused his stirring, sighed and then started again.

'Nobody has died, ya Layla,' he said quietly.

Layla frowned, walking into the kitchen and standing next to her father, breathing in the fumes of the *mulaa7*. The famous Sudanese red stew made with ground beef in a rich, spicy tomato sauce could be eaten either with *kisra*, a delicious thin savoury pancake cooked on flat hot plates, or *aseeda*, which was like a jelly bread made of sorghum flour.

There was no *aseeda* today though, there was only Baba, standing over a pot of *mulaa7* with a drawn, tired look on his face.

'What's wrong, Baba?' Layla asked, starting to worry.

Kareem stopped stirring and put his hand on his daughter's shoulder, leading her to the couch in the living room. 'Have a seat, *habiba*,' he said gently, then pulled a chair from the dining table and placed it in front of her. He settled into the seat, lifting his thick black-frame glasses and rubbing his face before sliding them back into place and refocusing on Layla.

'Habooba Samira, your mother's mama, is very sick. She's collapsed and is in the hospital. We're going to Khartoum tomorrow to be with her in this difficult time.'

WHAT?

'Go pack your bags. We're going to Sudan on the first flight out in the morning.'

Layla stared at her father, the words not quite sinking in.

Did he just say, we're going to Sudan? Tomorrow? Habooba collapsed? She's in hospital?

Layla shook her head, unable to process what she was hearing.

How could her grandmother – the strong, tall, powerful woman she remembered from their last family trip to Sudan, whose dark skin gleamed and shimmered when she walked, who had a witty reply to every sentence and a meal ready for everyone who walked through the door – be sick? Layla's imagination raced, envisaging the worst. Her grandmother with hundreds of tubes plugged into her body. Habooba, with machines around her beeping away, their sounds getting faster and faster and louder and louder. Habooba, with her eyes closed and her breathing heavy and her skin dull, robbed of its glow. *No, not Habooba. It can't be!* Ya Allah.

'Layla? Layla, *mashayti wayn, habiba*?' her dad asked.

Layla's eyes refocused on her father still sitting in front of her with worry etched across his face.

'No, no, no, I don't believe it. Not Habooba,' she blurted out. 'It can't be. We were just talking to her on the phone a few days ago. It can't be true.' Then, suddenly, surprising her father and herself, Layla started talking about her invention competition. 'What about the GDT? The international Grand Designs Tourismo is now a few months away. I can't just up and leave. I got selected for the SIIT today, and I'm supposed to be going to Germany, to France, to Ethiopia, to China. We've never been anywhere but to Sudan before. I'm supposed to, to, to . . .'

Layla wasn't really thinking as she spoke, the words again falling out of her mouth before she could even process them, her brain playing catch-up.

Her father shook his head. '*Inshallah khair*. We don't know any more details, ya Layla. Mama just needs to get over there now, and we need to support her,' he said gently, before his tone became firm. 'You're coming with us, Grand Designs Tourismo competition or not. This is a non-negotiable.'

'But I have to be here to work on the invention for the GDT! If I don't go to the meetings, I'll get kicked off the team, Baba. You don't want me to get kicked off the team, do you?'

'Layla, *khalas*. Stop this selfish behaviour. *Yallah*, go pack.' Kareem was resolute.

Layla's mind was still scrambling to make sense of this massive news. 'When will we be back, at least, so I can tell everyone? What should I say to Mr Gilvarry?' Layla asked, desperate as she sunk lower into the couch, her eyes glazing over.

'We don't know when we will be back. It might be better for you to tell the GDT that you're no longer part of the team, ya Layla. It's now time to focus on family. The GDT and the SIIT will be there next year, *Inshallah*. *Amshy*, go do some prayers for your grandmother and pack, *yallah*.' Kareem patted his daughter's knee, and then got up to leave.

Layla recoiled in shock.

Did he just say no more GDT?! No SIIT?!

Layla started to splutter with indignation, but her father had already left. *What is going on?* This was *not* the way she expected the evening to pan out.

The twins walked over to their sister and quietly sat on either side of her, each taking one of her hands and patting it gently. Layla grimaced, processing what had just happened.

I can't quit.

No, she would figure out a way to make it work. She knew what was best for herself. She always did, right? She couldn't give up everything now.

'It's okay, Layla,' the twins said, almost in unison.

'We can help you pack,' said Yousif.

'We've already finished packing our bags,' Sami added.

Layla wondered what they had put in their suitcases. Probably more Lego than clothes. A smile flickered across her face, but she caught herself and scowled again. Her grandmother was in hospital, Kareem wanted her to quit the GDT and she might have to give up the SIIT. This wasn't a time for smiling. She was going to need a plan.

After a few beats, Layla relented. 'Okay, *ya shabab*, show me the way.'

The young brothers jumped into action, sliding off the couch with the serious demeanour of children on a mission. Sami and Yousif marched their sister up the stairs, and Layla followed, still thrown for a loop.

At least I'll get to eat some aseeda *in Sudan at Habooba's house. But . . . will Habooba Samira even be well enough to cook?* The thought was little comfort.

'Can you believe we're going to Sudan tomorrow?' Sami whispered to his sister as they walked towards their bedroom. His voice sounded tentative, unsure.

Layla nodded. 'You don't remember Sudan, do you?' she said.

The twins shook their heads.

'We were babies last time,' Yousif offered.

Layla remembered it well. They hadn't even been able to walk yet.

'You boys were just little gurgling blobs,' Layla attempted to joke, and they both rewarded her with a giggle.

'Do you like Sudan?' Sami asked.

Layla paused, reflecting. 'I love the food, getting to hang with all the cousins, going to the market and buying fireworks,' she said, and her younger brothers smiled. 'But it's a bit complicated there sometimes,' she added, thinking of when her cousins mocked her accent, or her outfit, or her interests as not being Sudanese enough. 'With Habooba Samira sick this isn't going to be the usual holiday either,' she said.

Sami and Yousif instantly sobered, nodding in understanding.

Layla sat down on the floor of their bedroom, picking at the fibres of the grey carpet. Sami and Yousif started bringing her things they thought she should pack. As Yousif handed Layla the fifth yellow scarf in a row, she smiled sadly and motioned for them to sit next to her, coming in for a cuddle.

'What's Habooba really like?' asked Yousif, his voice muffled.

'She's my favourite,' Layla gushed. 'She's strong and feisty, and even though she does think that cooking is the best way to find a husband, she also thinks women should be allowed to do whatever they want. She's the ultimate boss. She's also funnier than Sami on Ribena. You'll love her!'

That night in bed, Layla texted Dina.

Layla
Dude, my grandma is in hospital.

Dina
What happened? She OK? You OK?

Layla
Nah, it's all a bit cooked. Flying to Sudan morow morn.

Dina
RU kidding?! Sad face.

Layla
And dad wants me to quit the GDT!

Dina
WOT that's wild. You can't! Didn't you say you just got picked for the SIIT too?

Layla
Yeh . . . but he doesn't care. I dunno what to do.

Dina
You'll figure it out, I'm sure bb.

Layla
Can you tell the boys? I'm too wrecked now to text anyone else.

Dina

Gotchyou, sis. Love you.

Layla

ily. Bye bibz.

Layla switched off her phone, stuffing it underneath her pillow. She spun around in bed, burying her face in the cotton pillowcase and doing her best to ignore the swarm of eels writhing around in the pit of her stomach. The thought of her favourite grandmother lying still and sick in hospital was too frightening to think about.

Maybe if I pray hard enough, Allah *will protect her*.

Layla wasn't sure if prayers really worked that way, but it was worth trying. Sneaking out of the top bunk, she lightly landed on her feet and rummaged in the corner of the room for her prayer scarf. She still had *wudhu* from her evening prayers so she was all ready to go. Very quietly, Layla rolled out the *muslaya* in the direction of Mecca. Wrapping her headscarf around her head, she stood on the foot of the mat, raised her hands to her ears and began to pray. As she murmured the words of *Al-Fatiha*, the opening verse of the Quran, a calm began to gently descend over her.

Breathe, she reminded herself. *In the name of* Allah, *breathe*.

CHAPTER 6

LAYLA had been back to Sudan before, Kareem and Fadia believing it was important that the kids stay connected to their culture. But the last time they'd been to Khartoum was five years ago: she had still been a kid. She didn't know what to expect this trip, but there was no time to dwell. The family was up early and on their way to the airport at the crack of dawn. Layla barely registered her surroundings as the family stood in queue after queue and eventually boarded the plane for the first leg of their flight.

'Look how big these screens are, Layla.' The twins were beside themselves with excitement at getting a TV each, playing with the screen on the back of the seat in front of them. The unlimited range of shows and games kept Layla and her siblings entertained for the duration of the thirteen or so hours to the brightly lit high-rise city in the Middle East.

Briefly, Layla could forget they were flying back to Sudan to see her sick grandmother. In the confines of the airplane, she could pretend she was anyone, going anywhere. *This is what it will be like when I'm going to Paris!* The thought brought a smile to her face, and made her even more sure that she needed to figure out a way to keep the SIIT and GDT plans on track.

'Tea or coffee?' the flight attendant asked Fadia and Kareem, who both asked for tea.

'Coffee, please,' said Sami, as he extended his short little arm holding a plastic white cup.

The Scandinavian flight attendant tittered, looking at Fadia.

Their mum shook her head. 'Juice only,' she said, and Sami didn't know the difference.

The second leg of the flight was full of Sudanese

travellers either visiting family or returning from holiday. Everyone on the plane talked about going home.

Home.

Layla wasn't sure whether Sudan was home, really. She liked going back to Sudan, but 'home' didn't really feel like the right description. Some parts of it felt 'homely' – like stories around the dinner table with Habooba Samira, being told off by *3ama* Bilqees for climbing over the house walls, giggling with her cousin Yousra over boardgames and Bollywood films, smiles and sweets from the neighbours. But did all of those things together make a home? And if Sudan wasn't home, did it make her not Sudanese?

'Do you feel like Sudan is home?' she asked Ozzie, interrupting him from a game.

He looked at her, annoyed. 'Nah, it's not. It's where we are from, that's all.' Ozzie turned his attention back to his game.

So unhelpful, wow. Where we are from? Layla had always told people that she was from Brisbane. *Sigh.* What use were older brothers, anyway?

'What about you, Baba?' she asked her father, who was listening in on their conversation.

Kareem sighed. 'Sudan will always be home for Mama and me, *habiba*. You kids have to decide on home yourselves.'

Decide ourselves? Seems like a lot of responsibility.

Layla slept for the four or so hours from Dubai to the Sudanese capital, Khartoum. As the plane's wheels made smooth contact with the runway, Layla was jolted awake by the thud. The whispers of hundreds of '*Alhamdulilahs*' filling the air, prayers of thanks to God for their safe arrival. Being surrounded by people who said the same things as her made Layla wonder if that was what home felt like.

People started standing up and clapping, smiling and talking to each other about Sudan's bright future. *That's weird.* Layla didn't remember that happening last time they flew to Sudan. She looked over at her brothers, who had also stood up and joined in with the clapping. Sami and Yousif weren't going to be much help, but maybe Ozzie could explain.

'What's going on?' Layla asked.

'Celebrating the revolution,' Ozzie replied, in the most genuinely nice tone Layla had *ever* heard him use, like, *ever.*

I don't know what he's talking about, but this revolution thing must be pretty magical if it can make too-cool-for-school Ozzie sound nice!

Fadia was on the phone almost immediately, switching off airplane mode, putting in a new sim card and calling her siblings. '*Ah-ha ya shabab, e7na wa9alna,*' she heard her mother say to someone, presumably the eldest of the siblings, Marwan.

Folks all around them were calling their family members, reporting that they had landed safely, catching up on the news, gossiping about the flight. Layla pondered on the cultural difference of people calling rather than texting as she went to check her phone, then remembered she didn't have a Sudanese sim, so couldn't get any messages. Kissing her teeth, she watched the digital clock on her screen tick over to midnight in Sudan, and a new day in Australia. Layla sighed and wondered what she had missed while she was in the air.

Without a working phone to distract her, Layla craned her neck to see over the seats, taking everything in. The plane was full of families. There were men of all sizes, ages and shades wearing white *jalabeeyas*, topped with a *3imma* – the large, white, classically Sudanese turban on their heads. The women almost all wore colourful *toubs*, complementing their outfits with henna-decorated hands and feet. Some of the women appeared to have dipped the tips of their fingers in dark red ink, while others had exquisite black patterns of flowers and shapes drawn all over their arms and feet, like the patterns on walls of the most beautiful mosques. Kids were dressed in their 'travel best', in cute suits and puffy dresses, all prim and proper for the long journey.

Layla could not have been in a more different environment than the GDT team meeting she had gone to less than forty-eight hours prior. *Wild*.

Fadia hurried the family off the plane, ushering everyone quickly down the stairs, the darkness of the night broken by flickering lights on the handrails and runway. Ozzie and Baba each carried one of the twins asleep on their back as they got onto the bus that would take the travellers from the aircraft to the terminal. The loud, diesel machine, covered in light brown Sahara dust, filled up quickly, the Hussein family huddling around their hand luggage in the middle of the crowded vehicle. There were no aerobridges here, no easy air-conditioned passenger walkway connecting the boarding gate to the plane.

The bus rumbled along towards the familiar airport building as Layla breathed in the hot, dusty air. In her tight jeans and oversized shirt, her loosely wrapped headscarf style and black sneakers, she wasn't dressed much like anyone else on the bus, though her headscarf style and facial features fit right in. Layla gazed up at her mother dressed in a dark blue textured *toub* and standing, as she always did, tall and proud among the passengers. Her mama seemed like she belonged, no matter where she was and what she wore. Layla noticed her mother's fierce grip on the handrail, skin stretching tightly over her knuckles. Mama was more worried about Habooba than she would ever say. *Oh* Allah, *please keep Habooba safe!*

Eventually, the bus stopped in front of a non-descript door to the main airport building and the passengers began to pour out, walking into a wide, open space with twenty or so counters smack bang in the middle of the hall. Only two of the counters were staffed: one signed 'SUDANESE' and the other signed 'FOREIGNER'.

Layla lazily began to follow the crowd, blinking her eyes as they adjusted to the brightness of the lights in the large hall. Her feet slowed to a stop, almost unconsciously.

What line am I meant to be in?

Ozzie, Mama, Baba and the twins had continued ahead towards the counters, swallowed up by the crowd. The rest of the passengers moved past Layla with increasing urgency. The teenager shut her eyes and tried to get her loudly beating heart to slow down. Layla wondered what was going on. It was just a standard customs line, what was the problem? Layla peered down at the passport in her hand, emblazoned with the Australian coat of arms – a kangaroo and an emu staring each other off over a shield. *It's funny how we eat our national animal*, she thought to herself absent-mindedly. But with this passport, which border line did she stand in, coming into the country of her birth?

Shaking her head and looking up, Layla sought out her family, who were standing in the foreigners' line. *Huh?* Even her mum and dad, who were clearly not *not Sudanese* were standing in the foreigners' line. *What is that about?* Pushing through the crowds of people milling about (there were no organised queue dividers here, so people stood wherever they liked), Layla headed to her family. Baba waved as she approached.

'Where did you go, *ya bit*?' Baba asked. 'We were searching for you. Were you in the *7amam*?'

'Nah, I wasn't on the loo – I don't like those squat toilets anyway,' Layla replied. 'I was just . . . admiring the design of the building.' Layla quickly made an excuse up. 'So exquisite.'

Ozzie, who was still carrying Sami on his back, surveyed the hall. The walls were bare, the ceiling was plain and there was nothing particularly significant about any of the features at all. Layla's older brother frowned slightly in confusion, but luckily for Layla, he kept quiet.

'Baba, why are we standing in the foreigners' line? I thought we were Sudanese?'

Kareem's face twitched imperceptibly, then he smiled. 'Ah yes, *tab3n* we are Sudaniya. We always will be. But coming in on the Australian passport makes it a lot quicker.'

'Oh,' Layla said uncertainly.

'*Yallah*, *shoofy!* See how short this line is compared to the other line?'

Her dad was right. The Sudanese line was snaking out the door, and there were only a handful of people in the foreigners' line.

'But –' *It couldn't be that simple, right?*

Ozzie sighed. 'Layla, right now is not the time,' he groaned, back to his surly self. 'It's late, we're all tired, and this was the shorter line, okay? It's not that deep.'

'*Mafi mushkilla, habibi.* We can talk about it later,' her father added.

Layla nodded reluctantly, wondering if she was making a big deal out of nothing. She felt tired, hungry and a little out of place, and they hadn't even made it into the city yet.

'Layla, do you want to fill your paperwork out?' Baba asked his daughter, attempting to distract her from pouting at the ground, picking at her short fingernails. At Baba's suggestion, she perked up, nodded and fished a pen out of her backpack. Kareem handed her the form on a thin sheet of pink paper.

'Should I write in English or Arabic?' Layla asked.

'Up to you, *habiba*,' he responded, before turning his attention to Yousif stirring from sleep still on his back.

Layla's eyes bulged, and she grimaced. *Hmm. Filling in this paper in Arabic will be a struggle, but surely this will show I fit in here, right? Right. Arabic it is!*

A few minutes later, the Hussein family reached the front of the customs line and the bored hijabi woman behind the counter ushered them over. Her perfectly made-up face could not have been more uninterested, and she motioned for Kareem to present the passports and paperwork using only a single eyebrow.

Wow, that's quite a skill!

Layla made a mental note to work on her eyebrow muscles later. Who knew you could show such a wide range of emotions with a mere strip of hair? *Subhanallah.* True goals!

The customs official flicked through the paperwork rapidly, glancing at each and making a few cursory ticks here and there. When she got to Layla's paper however, she paused. A smirk flickered across her face.

'*Dibita3tik?*' she said in Layla's direction.

Layla nodded wordlessly and held her breath. *What have I done this time?*

CHAPTER 7

THE customs official held eye contact with Layla for a moment then her face broke into a caustic smile. She crossed out all of Layla's entries, rewriting everything in English. 'Nekest time, Engileesy, okay?' she said, in accented English. 'Your handwriting is like a child!'

Layla's face burned with embarrassment, as Ozzie cackled beside her.

'Why do you always make it so hard on yourself, sis?' he teased. 'Get over it, we're all coconuts.'

The humiliation was complete. Layla felt like she was going to spontaneously combust in shame, any second now.

'I'm not a coconut,' she whispered fiercely right back. 'I'm a wombat!'

Ozzie laughed rudely.

Stuff Ozzie!

Smarting, she scanned her family for backup. Her mother wasn't paying attention, intensely involved in a conversation about her own mother on the phone. The twins were still asleep. Kareem, the only one listening, smiled at the customs lady appreciatively, then gave Layla's shoulder a kind squeeze.

'*Mafi mushkilla, habibi,*' he soothed. 'We can take some Arabic lessons, if you want, while you are here. It's all about practice.'

'I don't want Arabic lessons!' Layla was annoyed that it was being made *her* problem. 'What about what Ozzie said?'

'Ignore your older brother. He has his own path, okay?'

Layla sighed, resigned. Her Arabic was fine and pretty cool in Australia, where barely anyone else knew the Sudanese Arabic her family spoke. She could just say '*Alhamdulilah*' and people would be impressed. Here, though, that wasn't going to cut it. Layla's head throbbed, swirling with fatigue.

I forgot how awful jet lag is . . .

Passports stamped, Layla and her family walked through the gates and into the main area of the airport. Three large baggage carousels chugged sluggishly on each side of the hall, with two rows of luggage trolleys lazily snaking through the middle like a couple of well-fed pythons. Three thin men in dark blue overalls approached them quickly, jogging alongside empty luggage trolleys.

'*Ta3al ya zoul*,' they called to Baba and Ozzie, even motioning to Mama and Layla. They were some of the many street workers in Khartoum, people doing whatever they could to earn a few jineh (the Sudanese currency) and feed their family. Layla could see a sharp look in the eyes of everyone who approached them, asking the Husseins if they could help with the luggage, asking if they needed someone to walk with them to the car, asking if they needed a ride home, asking anything. Some, once rejected, would move onto another group, and others were more insistent, until a curt word uttered by Baba ended the conversation. Layla didn't know whether to feel annoyed by them, sorry for them or impressed with their hustle. She watched them get rejected over and over again by folks who had just flown in from other continents. It didn't feel right, to dismiss them so harshly for just doing their job, but she didn't know what to do about it.

The family finally reached the correct baggage carousel and stood a few meters back from the horde of people all suffocating the conveyor belt.

'*Yallah, ya shabab!*' Kareem said, sliding Yousif off his back and waking him up.

Ozzie also dislodged Sami from his back, gently placing the boy on his own two feet. Sami and Yousif turned to each other and hugged, both in affection and to keep each other upright. Layla smiled at their cute figures, all thick jumpers and messy curls. Ozzie and Kareem quickly walked off together, securing empty trolleys and bringing them back to where the family waited, before diving into the melee to retrieve their luggage. The bags looked slightly worse for wear, and it was obvious that they had been opened and checked, but apart from that, all was fine.

Finally, finally, it was time to get out of the airport. The Husseins pushed the trolleys through the short duty-free area, and then into the incredibly loud and crowded arrival hall. It was like walking into a wall of colour, noise and heat.

'We finally made it!' Layla piped up. 'Welcome to Sudan, little brothers.' She looked down at Sami and Yousif, their eyes wide, taking everything in.

'So many people, Layla,' Sami said quietly, gazing up at his sister, who nodded and smiled, clasping his hand.

'Yaaaaa Fadia!' a voice shouted from somewhere at the back of the room.

'FADIA!'

'KAREEEEEM!'

'*E7na hina!*'

They had been spotted. Out of the crowd, two individuals stood, waving. One was Mama's brother, Marwan – a tall, lean, olive-skinned man in a crisp white *jalabeeya*. The other was Kareem's sister, Bilqees – a short, stout, dark-skinned woman wearing a blue and yellow *toub*.

Kareem turned to regard his family. '*Yallah!* We will meet them *barra.*'

As they walked through the cacophony of the arrival hall and stepped into the outside courtyard, Layla took a large, deep belly breath.

Take it all in, gurl. You're back in Sudan!

Palm trees lined the courtyard dotted with people standing around and talking on their phones or idly waiting, leaning up against walls and pillars. The carpark stretched in front of the small bricked area, rows upon rows of dusty Toyotas and Hyundais, all rebranded to slightly unusual Sudanese names. The cars sat under an enormous canvas roof, protection from the hot Sahara sun. There was a thin layer of desert dust coating everything, and although it was in the middle of the night – and winter – the digital screen on the wall still indicated it was 32 degrees Celsius.

32 degrees! Raaaaaaaah.

Layla turned to ask Ozzie a question, but before she could get a word out, Marwan and Bilqees arrived, cousins in tow.

Oh . . . where is everyone else?

The small greeting party was a sure sign that this trip would be different. Last time, it had felt like almost a hundred cousins had arrived at the airport, showering them with kisses, well wishes, exclamations about how they had changed and grown. This time, it was just their aunt and uncle and three of their closest cousins. *This is definitely no ordinary holiday . . .*

Ozzie immediately gravitated towards the family's older set of twins: the seventeen-year-old

Ma'ab and Mohammed. The boys hugged and clasped each other's hands in greeting. Layla made eye contact with her closest cousin, Yousra, the younger sister of Ma'ab and Mohammed. *Oh, Yousra!* They both ran towards each other.

'Ya Layla, *habiba*, *waaawww*, it's so good to see you,' Yousra cooed to her cousin in greeting, her warm voice muffled by Layla's scarf material as they hugged.

'Yousra, *habiba*! It's been so long. What, years?'

'Five years, *habiba*, since I've got to hug you and squeeze you and give you a big kiss.' Yousra gave Layla a smooch on the cheek. '*Wa7ashteena!* I've missed you so much!'

'I know. You don't like my voice notes?' Layla joked.

'Social media isn't the same, *habiba*.' Yousra smiled knowingly. 'Plus, there's so much I want to tell you.'

'Ahhhh, I can't wait, but seriously. Look at you! You're like a proper woman now, *Mashallah*.'

Yousra was *radiant*. Nothing had prepared Layla for how much Yousra had changed in person. She was less young teen and more *woman,* even though at fifteen, she was only a year older than Layla. Her hijab was worn in the traditional Sudanese manner, the silky material perfectly framing her sculpted face. Her cream skirt flowed around her ankles like water over smooth stone, and the pale pink blouse on top was gently ruffled at the sleeves, elegantly framing her delicate wrists. Yousra's brown eyes, unusually flecked with green and gold, twinkled. Their cheeky mischievousness felt like the only thing that was more suited to her fifteen-year-old self. Layla was taken aback by how much her cousin had changed. Layla was just the same old Layla!

Yousra then broke the hug and held Layla back by the shoulders to inspect her properly. 'My Australian cousin. You haven't changed a single bit.'

Layla chuckled hesitantly. *The 'Australian' cousin?* The thought of the customs line popped up again.

'Yeh, you know. I might not appear to be different, but my soul has been transformed!'

Yousra's smile faltered and a slight confused frown coloured her face.

'Okay . . .'

Layla scolded herself for the terrible gag, then tried to recover. *Janey Mack, my jokes do NOT translate here.* 'Nah, jokes, *habiiiiiib*,' Layla went back to safer ground. 'I'm just happy to be in Sudan, even though it's for a sad reason.'

Yousra's face dropped as they both took in the sombre nature of the trip. Yousra wrapped her arm into Layla's, comfortingly. '*Inshallah*, Habooba will be okay.'

'Were you with her? What happened?'

Yousra shook her head. 'I was coming home from school, and she apparently collapsed, *wa khalas*. They said it might be a stroke, but I have no idea what that means.'

A stroke? What's a stroke? Layla sucked in a deep breath, coughing slightly with the dry air. 'She'll be okay. Mama's here now too, so she will help, right?'

Yousra nodded, the lightheartedness of the moments earlier completely forgotten. 'Oh, I'm so happy that you're here now,' Yousra whispered. 'It's . . .'

Even though Yousra didn't say it, Layla knew exactly what she meant. *It's scary when you don't know what's going to happen.*

'*Yallah, al-mustashfa?*' Fadia interrupted, keen to head straight to the hospital to see her mother. Her usually composed face was creased with worry and fatigue, her *toub* had rumpled and she looked weighed down with the strain of what was ahead.

A still quiet hung over the group. Khalu Marwan, the eldest on Fadia's side of the family, quickly took charge.

'Habooba is at Al-Faisal hospital, next to al-Souq al-Arabi,' he said.

'*Tamam,* I'll go with you now,' said Fadia to her brother, and Baba nodded with confirmation.

'We can go to Bahri and settle in for the night,' suggested Kareem.

'Just make sure you avoid the main protest areas,' Marwan replied.

Protest areas? What was he talking about? Did this have something to do with why they were clapping on the plane?

Layla turned to Yousra to clarify, but the conversation had already moved on.

'*Ara7,*' Baba said to his kids, ushering them towards the car. 'Mama will meet us at home when she's done.'

'Should we go and see Habooba too?' Ozzie asked his father, a crease on his brow that Layla hadn't seen before.

'We can all visit her in the morning. Right now, let's just get some rest.'

Layla looked to Yousra, but her cousin had peeled off to the side, staring at her phone, murmuring under her breath. What was she doing? Layla noticed a white cord slinking up from Yousra's phone underneath her scarf and realised that she must be listening to something on her phone. *Is she talking to someone? So sneaky!*

'Yousra!' she called. Her cousin's eyes flicked up, and Yousra smiled without replying.

'See you at home?' Layla called, and Yousra nodded.

'*Yallah!*' Kareem called again, and with that, the four kids – a slightly agitated Ozzie, an emotionally drained Layla and two very tired twins in Sami and Yousif – followed their dad to Uncle Marwan's car. It was a four-door Toyota hilux ute, affectionately called *al-box*. The suitcases were slung into the open tray at the back, and then Baba turned to his kids.

'*Yallah*, who wants to sit in the back of *al-box* with the suitcases?'

Immediately, everyone perked up. 'ME!' all the kids shouted in unison, grabbing onto the sides of the tray, boosting themselves on the wheels of the truck, clambering over the metal sides and falling on top of the suitcases. Although there was a lot about Sudan that was complicated, this was one of the simple pleasures: travelling in Khartoum on the back of a ute, no seatbelts, the desert air in your face, yelling and waving as they flew down *Shari3 Al-Matar*. They had indeed, arrived.

CHAPTER 8

LAYLA started, waking herself up. The room was dark and the single bed she lay in felt unfamiliar. She reached down and felt the light sheet draped over her, a thin blanket rough on her fingers. Where was she? How had she got there? Layla scratched her head, stubby fingers fighting through knots to reach her scalp. The last thing she remembered was sitting in the back of a ute, breathing in the dry air as they crossed the Blue Nile Bridge, Tuti Island on their left, yelling exuberantly into the wind.

Oh, we're in Sudan! Layla smiled as she

remembered, wiggling in her soft cotton yellow *jalabeeya*. And it was morning, so she could catch the milkman too. Seed al-labn, *here I come! I can't wait to be a milkwoman again, riding the donkey and spreading the lactose.*

The local milkman, *3mu 3umar*, Layla remembered, would come around every morning on a grey donkey (Layla had named it Bolt). Sometimes, if he had enough time, *3mu 3umar* would let the kids jump on the back of the wooden platform he sat on and ride around the neighbourhood with him. It was like a Sudani carriage, but much less fancy than the ones in fairytales. Layla thought it was such a fun – and environmentally friendly – way to get around. *They really should consider it in Brisbane . . . though donkeys do poo quite a lot.*

Layla had always loved hanging out with *seed al-labn*, despite her aunties saying it wasn't what proper girls did. *What is a proper girl anyway?*

Then, just as suddenly as she woke, her face dropped. Layla's brain had slowly shifted into gear, reminding her why they had come to the country of her birth in the first place. Layla sighed, then looked at the digital clock on top of the cupboard.

The red light of the clock was blinking: 01:59, 01:59, 01:59.

Ya-nahr-abyad. If the light was blinking a strange time like that, it usually meant the electricity had gone out during the night. The electricity cut out every so often in Sudan, especially when it was really hot, and most people were using fans or air conditioning.

The bed creaked as Layla shifted her weight on the thin mattress and dropped her feet to the ground, tentatively searching for her *shibshib*. The floors were always covered in a thin layer of dust, no matter how hard you cleaned, so everyone wore slippers or thongs at all times. But thongs were exclusively *inside* shoes.

'Do you want people to think you are a beggar?' the aunties would ask admonishingly, if she even *thought* about going outside without 'proper' attire on her feet.

'What's wrong with beggars? They're people too,' Layla would retort, but that never quite convinced anyone.

Aunties can be so shady sometimes.

Layla quietly navigated her way around the room, sneaking towards the adjoining mini salon.

She passed the twins sharing a bed and wrapped up in each other's arms (they loved to hug when they went to sleep, it was adorable!), Ozzie in another bed and Yousra in the other. Ma'ab and Mohammed were sleeping outside. That was the way things worked in Sudan: everyone shared rooms, beds and lived on top of one another.

The mini salon was the heartbeat of the household, and it was also the room that connected all the main areas of the building. On one side was the kids' room, where Layla was sleeping with her siblings and cousin. On the other side was the adults room, where Khalu Marwan and his wife, Amal were sleeping. The mini salon then opened up to the main section of the house: a large space that included the guest salon, the dining table and an entry to the kitchen off to the side. A soft curtain of beads separated the mini salon from the main guest area, offering a bit of privacy in a house design that was decidedly public, like many other Sudanese houses in their neighbourhood.

In the mini salon, the analogue clock on the wall said it was just after 5.30 am. The large, circular timepiece ticked loudly in the silence. 5.30 am! Layla must be jet lagged. Changing time zone was the only reason Layla ever woke up so early.

Layla padded through the mini salon, careful not to wake up her mum and dad who were each sleeping on a *3angareb*. The *3angareb* was a special kind of Sudanese bed with a simple wooden frame and a grid of slender rope weaved together to make a comfortable surface for the thin mattress. Sudanese homes often had more *3angarebs* than people – they were for sitting and sleeping, for guests and for members of the household. There were three *3angarebs* in the mini salon; two where her parents were sleeping, and one on the back wall, together set in a U-shape. The back bed was Habooba's. It sat empty and untouched, a stark reminder that Layla's grandmother was in the hospital.

Sneaking through, Layla hurriedly slipped past the curtain of beads, into the main guest area.

What to do, what to do? Layla considered doing some GDT work while she waited for everyone to get up. She would have to find a way, somehow, to balance being in Sudan for her family and fulfilling her role in the GDT. Yes, technically, she wasn't supposed to be in the team any more. But she wasn't ready to quit the GDT and give up her spot on the international tour just yet. Layla hadn't officially resigned, or even told anyone apart from Dina and the boys that she had left the country, so if she kept the work up, maybe she could get away with it. Maybe she just wouldn't mention to Peter that she was in Sudan. Was that bad?

Hmm, I'm going to need to get internet first though.

Before she could figure out what to do, a loud noise echoed through the house. Layla froze before recognising the call and relaxing. She took a seat at the dining table and closed her eyes, murmuring the words under her breath as she heard them.

Allahu akbar, Allaaaaaahu akbar!

It was the morning call to prayer coming from the mosque across the road. *So good!* This wasn't a thin pre-recorded sound from the family computer speakers. This was a full-throated, hearty call to prayer, coaxing people out of bed, reminding the neighbourhood that prayer is better than sleep, encouraging the community to congregate. As the *mu'athin* uttered the last phrase of the call with a flourish, both Baba and Marwan came through

the bead curtain, wearing white *jalabeeyas,* ready
to head to the mosque. Layla's eyes flew open.

'*Sabah alkhair!*' she called, announcing a good
morning to her dad and uncle way too loudly for
any time of the day, let alone while everyone slum-
bered. Scrambling off the chair, Layla ran over
and wrapped her chubby arms around her uncle's
frame.

Khalu Marwan gazed down affectionately
at his niece as she hugged him, chuckling. 'Ah,
someone woke up early,' he said.

'Can I come with you?' she asked in Arabic.

Khalu Marwan shook his head, and Layla
pouted. She had conveniently forgotten things
worked a bit differently in Sudan. 'This mosque
is small, ya Layla, and they don't have a section
for girls yet,' Marwan said. 'But *yallah*, why don't
you walk with us out to the mosque if you want?'

'*Mumkin?*' Layla addressed the question to
her dad, and he nodded, granting her permission.
Layla squealed, before quickly being hushed by
both men simultaneously.

'Everyone else is still sleeping, *ya bit*,' Kareem
said, and his daughter ducked her head and snickered as she let go of her uncle to get ready.

She rushed past the bead curtain into the bedroom, rifling through her suitcase for an *abaya* in the dark. Yousra stirred, but no one woke up.

'*Yallah*, ya Layla. We have to go,' Kareem called.

Hurriedly getting ready, Layla ran out of the room and followed her dad and uncle down the patio steps, past the ute and through the front gate. *I can't believe I'm here*. As they walked, Layla took a mental picture. She peered at the windy alley before her, squinting in the dark at the potholes and mud puddles as far as the eye could see, clay water urns held by black metal frames in front of most houses for passers-by who were thirsty. A stray dog and cat hobbled by, shuffling like wounded soldiers off a battlefield. As they reached the end of the street and her father and uncle peeled off towards the mosque, she could see the open area that was used as a football field, rubbish scattered across the plain, and on the left, a stream of people trickling towards the *masjid*. Layla took in a deep breath. The early morning breeze was still cool, and a dewy moisture hung in the air. Ah, Sudan!

Placing her hands on her hips, and turning back towards the house, Layla thought about what to do next. She could wait at the gate for *seed al-labn* to come or go for a walk around the neighbourhood or . . . *yikes*! She should probably finish the minutes from the last GDT meeting before Peter started to chase her again.

With that thought in mind, Layla snuck back into the house and found her school iPad. In the quiet, among the snores of Ozzie and the light whistling of Yousra's breathing, she started putting together the notes from the last GDT meeting. She needed to get it done before her dad got back and found her working on it. But there was one big problem.

I have no idea how I am going to email this without internet. I need to ask Yousra about getting access.

But if she could get it done in the next few hours, no one would suspect a thing, right? *Inshallah!*

Not long after she finished writing up the minutes for the GDT, Layla heard the men return from the *fajr* prayers and their morning walk. She still hadn't heard *seed al-labn* come around yet, so she snuck back out to the mini salon to see what was going on. The household was starting to come alive; Amal was in the kitchen preparing tea while Marwan and Kareem were sitting at the dining table reading the morning's newspapers. Layla jumped up on a chair to join them.

'What's new?' she asked her dad, who had his nose buried in that morning's copy of *Al-Sudani*.

Kareem grunted, but didn't reply.

Sami and Yousif wandered in and Layla turned into big sister mode. 'Boys, have you brushed your teeth?' she asked semi-sternly. Shaking their heads, Layla looked pointedly at them, and they begrudgingly turned around and trudged to the bathroom.

Layla tried to get some conversation going again, this time with her uncle. 'What's new, Khalu Marwan?'

'It's all news about the revolution, Layla,' he replied. 'Have you been following it?'

Layla shook her head. She didn't really follow politics.

'Sudanese people want a new government, so they are going out to the streets to demand it. You have protests in Australia too, *mushkida*?'

Layla wrinkled her nose, thinking about it. She'd seen people go out into the streets to march for things like Invasion Day, but that seemed different. These demonstrations weren't like the Women's March either, though Layla couldn't quite put her finger on why. *Hmm . . .*

'Can't you just wait and vote for a new government?' Layla wondered. Voting days in Australia were so much fun, and the best thing was the sausage sizzles. *What would a Sudani sausage sizzle be like? Maybe they have* agasheh! 'Is the revolution like a long voting day?'

Marwan chuckled. 'We don't have voting days like you do in Australia, Layla. That's what people want, the chance to freely vote for anyone, and preferably not someone in the military.'

'That's enough politics for now,' Kareem piped up from behind the papers, before Layla had a chance to ask another question. 'Layla, go help your aunty.'

Layla rolled her eyes and jumped off the chair to join her aunty in the kitchen.

'What's going on, *Khaltu*? Baba is being weird. Also, when is *seed al-labn* getting here? I want to go around the *7ila* with him.'

Amal let out a long exhale, as she prepared the coffee and tea over the stove. 'There's no *seed al-labn* these days, ya Layla. Things have all stopped since the protests began a few months ago. Times are changing, *habiba.*'

Hmm. I thought the biggest change was going to be Habooba's health, but things seem a bit more complicated.

'While you're here, do you mind taking this tray out to the table?' Amal asked Layla.

Layla chuckled to herself. Of course she would end up with chores if she walked into the kitchen. Nodding, Layla lifted the silver tray, heavy with pots and glasses, and took them to the men sitting at the dining table before deciding to see what else was happening around the house.

Layla found Ma'ab on the patio with a variety of bits and pieces in front of him. The tall and lanky Sudani teenager frowned in concentration, his slicked back curls glinting in the sunlight.

'What are you up to, Ma'ab? Are you making something?'

'Yeh, I'm putting together some posters for the protest later and then I'll be doing a service on *al-box.*'

Ma'ab trailed off as he concentrated on screwing in the wood to the thick poster card. Layla stood there, watching. She didn't know anyone else in the family liked making stuff.

'Mohammed paints them and I put them together,' he said. 'Teamwork.'

'Can you tell me more about the protests?' Layla asked, her curiosity piqued.

'Everyone is out on the streets because they want a new president, and going out on the streets is the only way we can get one. This president has been terrible for Sudan, for all of us.' Ma'ab took his eyes off the thick poster card, catching the frown scratched across his younger cousin's face. 'Don't worry, it's been very peaceful,' he said reassuringly.

'And you've been joining them?' Layla asked.

Ma'ab nodded. 'Every day now. Mohammed and I go together.'

'Is it scary?'

Ma'ab sucked in a deep breath and his eyes flickered over the horizon.

'What we're fighting for isn't scary, and that's the important thing, *mushkida*?'

Layla shrugged, suddenly self-conscious. She

hadn't really thought about needing to fight for anything *political* before. But then Layla thought about the woman she'd seen at the Brisbane airport wearing a T-shirt with the Aboriginal flag on the front, and 'Always was, always will be' on the back, and the conversations she'd had with her Turrbal teacher, Ms Taylor, during class. Maybe Sudan wasn't the only place that needed to fight for justice, that needed revolution. *But I'm just a school kid, what can I do?*

'Well, then, do you want to help me?' Ma'ab asked in the silence of Layla's thoughts.

Layla's face broke into a grin. Making things, *that* she knew about. 'Yes, please! You know I recently learned to TIG weld aluminium?'

'Oh wow, *Mashallah,* lil cuz. That's pretty impressive. Fancy, too. I've only ever used MIG. So, you're handy with the tools, mmm?'

Layla nodded enthusiastically. *Finally, someone who appreciates my skills!*

'*Yallah.* I want all these wooden bits attached to the posters here. Then we'll change the oil in *al-box* so we'll be ready for the day, *tamam?*' Ma'ab handed Layla some wooden bits and a screwdriver, and pointed at the card and screws.

'And if you're really good, I'll show you something I've been working on in the back shed. I'm fixing this old generator. Maybe you can give me a hand with that too, *tamam*?'

Layla beamed. *Looks like Ma'ab also loves fixing and building things! Must run in the family, hehe.*

This might not be the GDT, but at least she was building stuff. This will keep Layla busy and her skills sharp while she was away. *Tamam* indeed!

CHAPTER 9

AFTER a while of screwing cardboard and wood together, Layla was ready for a break – and some Sudanese tea. As she walked into the house to wash her hands, she noticed Habooba's empty bed again.

'Baba, when are we going to see Habooba?' she asked her father, who was still at the dining table reading the paper.

Kareem sighed and faced his daughter, smoothing his hand over his hair – one, two, three times. 'Let's go see if your mother is up then we can start making plans, *Inshallah*.'

Two hours later *(gotta love Sudani time!)*, they were piling into the ute, heading to the hospital. Ozzie, Ma'ab and Mohammed went in the back tray of the ute, and Yousra, Sami, Yousif and Layla got in the back seat.

'What is all that you're bringing with you?' asked Fadia from the passenger seat, as Ma'ab, Mohammed and Ozzie tried to subtly smuggle protest placards onto the tray of the ute. Fadia was not in the best mood this morning, which was understandable given her mother was in hospital.

Layla figured if she was nice and helpful, it might make her mama feel better. 'Those are the protest things we made this morning,' Layla offered, before she heard Ma'ab's *'Shhhh!'*. It was too late.

'You boys want to join the protest today?' Fadia kissed her teeth. 'With Habooba in hospital?'

Oh dear. Maybe that wasn't the way to cheer her up.

Fadia's eyes burned with disappointment. 'Marwan, did you agree to this?' she asked her brother, who was sitting in the driver's seat.

Marwan sighed. 'Leave them, they've been sitting with their grandmother for days.'

Fadia frowned, Marwan's answer wasn't what she was expecting. She turned back to the boys. 'Ozzie, you're coming with us to the hospital.'

'But, Mama!'

'*La*. We're in Sudan to visit your grandmother and you're coming with us. End of story.'

'Getting to the hospital will take a little longer than usual,' Marwan said, eyeing his sister. 'The protests happening around the city are causing a bit of traffic.'

Fadia kissed her teeth again.

Layla eyed her mum, not quite understanding. 'Why don't you like the protests, Mama? Aren't they a good thing? I thought this president was bad,' she asked. Layla was curious about her mother's reaction to what was clearly the main news in town.

Marwan looked at his sister, also waiting to hear the perspective of a Sudanese woman who left the country a long time ago.

'Did the last five protests work?' Fadia asked Layla, who shrugged in response. Her mum answered her own question. 'No, they didn't.

People have been trying to get rid of this man for a long time. All that happens is that people we love get hurt, and then nothing changes. *Khalas*.'

Layla's shoulders fell, unsure what to say next. Uncle Marwan answered for her. 'No, they didn't work, but we have to keep trying.'

Fadia was silent, so Marwan continued talking to his sister. 'Things are tough, ya Fadia, tougher than they ever have been. These kids taking to the street, they're giving us the hope that has been gone for a long time.' As Fadia shifted in her seat, Marwan went in for a final blow. 'But you wouldn't know, because you never visit, do you?' Tension filled the air between the siblings.

'You know why I left, Marwan. After what happened to Ola,' Fadia said.

'She would have wanted you to stay,' Marwan hit back.

'Don't tell me what my best friend would have wanted,' Fadia hissed.

Layla grimaced in the back seat. Things were getting awkward! *Time to jump in and break the ice.*

'Aw, nice to know you fight with your brothers just as much as I do, Mama,' Layla joked.

She was the only one who found it funny. The silence was suffocating.

Oh, ya Allah. *Please help people get my jokes. This lack of a laugh is making my heart hurt.*

Marwan drove through the house gate carefully, and Kareem waved goodbye to the family as he closed the large blue metal door behind them.

'*Bismillah,*' Marwan muttered under his breath, glancing at the kids in the back he asked if someone could do the prayer for travel.

Sami and Yousif had just learned the appropriate *duaa*, so they started reciting in unison. Layla's eyes glazed over as she focused on the other side of the window, hungrily taking in every detail she could see.

'What do you think of Sudan, ya Sami and Yousif?' she asked her little brothers after they had finished the *duaa*. The streets of Khartoum couldn't be more different to the leafy and ordered world of Brisbane, Australia.

'Everyone's clothes are different to Brisbane. They all dress like Mama,' Sami said.

Yes, there were all sorts out there – ladies in *toubs* and *abayas* and skirts and scarves; men in *jalabeeyas* and *3immas*, others in slacks and shirts.

'And so many dogs and animals on the street,' Yousif added. 'Are they people's pets?'

Layla shook her head. 'No, *habibi*. These are definitely not the pampered pooches of Brisvegas.'

Layla closed her eyes as she tried to make sense of the differences between Khartoum and Brisbane. Maybe it *was* the animals – the stray cats and dogs, all matted hair and carnivorous eyes; donkeys pulling timber carts and the occasional goat, which would probably eventually end up on someone's plate (they were really delicious though). Hmm, no . . . the difference wasn't just the Muslim-friendly outfits, or the potted roads, or the hectic traffic, or the dusty air, or even the *athan* that went off five times a day, no. There was something more – *something* . . .

THUD! BAM! THUMP!

Layla was jolted out of her reverie by loud banging on the side of the car.

'What was that?!' Sami and Yousif both yelped, gawking at each other, then their sister.

Shaking her head and tuning into what was going on around them, Layla realised that the crowd they had been driving into wasn't just the usual morning market rush. It was the organised protest they had just been talking about, and people were thumping on their ute in the rush and excitement.

'It's okay, *ya shabab,* it's just people being passionate,' Layla reassured her younger brothers.

'Ya Baba!' Ma'ab called to his dad, Khalu Marwan, from the back. 'We're just going to get out here.'

Ma'ab and Mohammed jumped off the back of the ute and Ozzie joined them. Fadia whipped around.

'OZAIR, get back in the car, *now*! We're going to visit your grandmother!' she yelled.

'I'll be at the hospital soon, ya Mama. Don't worry,' Ozzie replied, then the three boys melted into the crowd, disappearing from view almost instantly.

Fadia muttered angrily under her breath. Layla hadn't heard her mum call him Ozair for years. She must be super angry.

'What do you –?'

'Layla, I don't want to hear a *word* out of you, okay?' snapped her mother.

Layla shut up, real quick. Sami and Yousif gaped at her, hands covering their mouths, stifling giggles.

Not funny! Layla glared at them, but that didn't stop their mirth.

Marwan continued to drive, slowly, honking to make his way through. People of all ages were milling around, some chanting, others holding signs, the crowd swelling and moving in the same direction.

After what seemed like years, he called from the front. 'We're almost there, *ya shabab*.'

A chill ran through Layla as the reality sunk in. Whatever the political situation, or her excitement at seeing Yousra, this situation was no fun at all. Her grandmother was sick and neither the GDT nor the SIIT prize was going to fix it. All Layla could do was pray.

CHAPTER 10

THE family rushed through the hospital as soon as they arrived, dashing past visitors and doctors and nurses, Layla barely able to register the pastel walls and antiseptic smell of the wards.

'You see how things are so rundown? And this is one of the best hospitals in the country,' Yousra said, as they hurried through the corridors. 'That's why we want a new president. The government is supposed to look after us, but they don't. They spend the money on themselves and leave us with nothing.'

'Did it always used to be like this?' Layla asked, wondering if this was the world her parents had grown up in.

Yousra shook her head. 'No, it's got much worse since you were last here.'

Layla nodded, understanding more and more. 'So, it's not just 'cos you don't like him, is it?'

'No,' Yousra said. 'We don't have a choice.' Layla's cousin fell silent. '*Yallah*, let's go. I'll fill you in later.'

As they reached the ward housing her grandmother, Layla's feet slowed. She didn't know how she felt about seeing her beloved grandma in bed, ill. She bit her lip then reached over and grabbed Yousra's hand. Yousra turned to Layla, slightly startled, then softened as she saw the expression on her cousin's face.

'I got you, *habiba*. I got you,' she said.

'I don't know how to do this,' Layla whispered back.

'Do what?'

'See Habooba. What am I meant to do, or say?'

This was a different type of challenge to facing up to Peter or being involved in the GDT. This wasn't a case of 'channelling the *jamel*'. In those cases, she just had to be strong for *herself*, fight things that she believed were wrong and ignore the barking dogs that were trying to distract her from continuing on her path. This? This was hard, because there was nothing she could do to change the situation.

'Just be yourself, *habiba*. Plus, your mum is here now, so she can help. Other than that, all we can do is pray.'

The words were meant to reassure Layla, but instead, they left her with an overwhelming feeling of helplessness.

C'mon, Layla, she told herself. *Be happy! Be brave! Be strong!* That's what she could do.

So, after the rest of the family had walked in to greet Habooba, Layla took a deep breath and bound into the room with a hop, skip, jump and smile.

'Haboobaaaaaaaa! Hiiii!!!' Her words came out a little too loudly.

There was no response. The silence was deafening.

'Habooba?' Layla asked again, this time quietly, her voice laced with uncertainty.

Fadia, who had taken her place in a chair in the back corner of the room, motioned for her daughter to come closer. She took Layla into her arms and enveloped her in a warm embrace, quietly murmuring reassuring noises. Yousra sat on a chair on the other side of the room, head bowed.

'Habooba is asleep right now,' Fadia said. 'We need to let her rest.'

Layla collapsed on her mother's lap. She hadn't been held like this by her mum in a long time, but it was what she needed right now to make her feel safe.

'Can she hear us when we talk?' Sami piped up from the other corner of the small, cramped space. His right hand was in his mouth, teeth chewing mindlessly on his fingers. It was a habit that showed up when he was nervous.

'Maybe, *habibi*, maybe. Why don't you try talking to her, or tell her a story?' Fadia said.

Sami gave his mother a quick nod before turning to his twin, motioning for Yousif to join him next to Habooba's bed. They both stared dolefully at their grandmother, her dark skin wax-like, giving her the appearance of a life-sized doll. A machine beeped behind her head, and tubes connected to her veins pulsed with liquid. Yousif took his grandmother's hand and began to calmly stroke it. Sami cleared his throat and began to tell a story that he had made up, about a crocodile in a swamp. Layla couldn't help but smile to herself. It wasn't the story she would choose to share with Habooba in this moment, but their grandmother, if she could hear, was probably chuckling too.

'And then the crocodile ate the man's foot,' Sami said triumphantly, ending his monologue and surveying the room proudly, as if for applause.

Yousif grinned widely at his twin, lightly clapping with his index fingers, so as not to wake his grandmother up. 'That was *mumtaz*!' he whispered proudly. They were such sweeties!

Layla got up and joined the twins at the side of the bed. 'How about we say some *duaas* for Habooba?' she asked them. 'Do you remember the *duaa* we say when we're visiting someone who is sick?'

Yousif nodded proudly. '*La ba'sa tahoorun Inshallah*,' Yousif recited quietly.

Sami repeated it and Layla joined in, as did Yousra. Soon, everyone in the room was pleading to their Lord under their breath, hoping that the matriarch would soon wake up.

After what seemed like an age, nurses walked into the room to give Habooba Samira her next round of medicine. As Layla watched the nurses and Fadia fuss about her grandmother, Layla's stomach groaned loudly. *When was the last time I ate?*

Fadia, hearing the rumbling thunder of Layla's empty stomach, looked over her shoulder.

'Why don't you and Yousra go get some snacks for everyone? Find something to stop that stomach rumbling so loudly, mmm?' Fadia said to Layla.

'Can we go too?' the twins asked.

Fadia shook her head, ignoring the younger boys' pouts. She fished some cash from a pocket somehow hidden in her *toub*, and shushed the girls out.

'How are you feeling now, Layla?' Yousra asked, as they walked out of the sombre room. 'It wasn't so bad, *mushkida*?'

Layla considered. 'Ah, I don't know. It's just so sad to see her like that, in the bed, helpless.'

Yousra hummed in acknowledgement. 'I know. But it's amazing your mum can speak to the doctors and make sure everything gets done right. Are you going to be a doctor like your mum?'

Layla shook her head, mildly surprised at the question. She'd never considered being a doctor before, really. 'Nah, people are so complicated. What, do you want to be a doctor?' Layla asked her cousin.

'Oh yes, *Inshallah*! Doctors make people's lives so much better.' Yousra's response was passionate. 'So, what do you want to do then?'

'I want to be an inventor!' said Layla.

'A what?'

Layla thought about how to explain her passion to her cousin as they continued to walk through the busy hospital corridors, looking for somewhere to buy snacks. 'You want to fix people, I want to fix problems. You know?'

'Like the government?'

'Hmm . . . not quite, but *ya3ni*.'

'Layla, if you're hiding something that could fix the government, you cheeky thin–' Yousra's phone started to ring and a boy's face popped up on the screen before she quickly declined the call.

Layla's eyes bulged. 'OMG, who was that?'

Yousra smiled, somehow demure and mischievous at the same time. 'Oh, you know . . .'

Layla playfully slapped her cousin's shoulder. 'No, I don't know, because you don't tell me anything.'

They both laughed, Layla a loud guffaw and Yousra a tinkling giggle, like a bell that rung when you entered a shop.

'Let me show you,' Yousra said, pulling up Instagram, fingers flying. '*Mi-jakisni,*' she said to Layla proudly, offering the phone like a trophy.

'Huh?' Layla replied, scrolling through the images. There were only a couple of his actual face, the rest were photos of sunsets on the Nile, random cars and trees.

'He's my boyfriend,' Yousra smiled, then quickly exited the app, taking the phone to the innocent wallpaper of a dew-covered rose.

A boyfriend? Yousra has a boyfriend?

Layla's recoiled at the news, her mind reeling. She couldn't quite believe it. Yousra was the 'perfect' Sudanese girl – they weren't supposed to have boyfriends, were they?

'I met Fareed on the gram . . .' Yousra explained.

On Instagram?!

'He is so mature . . .'

He's older?!

'We talk all the time . . .'

OMG, that's what she was doing on the phone at the airport!

'But I thought we weren't allowed to have boyfriends,' Layla said, interrupting the flow of Yousra's gushing.

Yousra paused, smiled coyly. 'Oh, you know how it is. Everyone does it anyway,' she replied smoothly in Arabic, and then continued on about the boy she was dating.

Do they? Does everyone do it? Do what, exactly?

Layla was taken aback, her head spinning like she'd just come off a high speed merry-go-round. If she was wrong about something as straight-forward as whether or not people like her and Yousra had boyfriends, how many other things was she wrong about?

Layla's head suddenly hurt. She dropped her face into both hands, massaging her temples, confused. Her mouth was dry and her throat throbbed. *I need to sit down for just a second . . .*

She spied two empty plastic chairs tucked away in a little alcove in the corridor and made a beeline for them. Yousra duly followed, not quite knowing what to do with her cousin's sudden change in behaviour. As they sat down, dust particles swirling around them, Layla looked at Yousra again.

'Whoa. It's a lot to take in, you know? I didn't think it was like that here, because so many people are Muslim and we Sudanese are supposed to do things differently to the *khawajaat*, that's what Mama and Baba always say.'

Yousra's lip curled up as she shook her head. 'Layla, don't people do this in Australia too? As if you don't do anything that breaks the rules,' she chuckled callously. 'It's not like you're fully Sudaniya anyway, so you might as well, right?'

Layla frowned. Not fully Sudaniya? She was just as Sudaniya as her cousin, wasn't she?

'That's a bit harsh, yeh,' Layla bit back, defending herself. 'I wear the right clothes, I speak Arabic and my blood is just as Sudanese as yours. I was born here, wasn't I?' Her voice hardened as she spoke, masking the deep hurt blooming across her chest. What made it worse was that Yousra did not seem to realise the impact of her words.

This whole trip was hurting her. Nothing was straightforward. Sudan was supposed to be simple.

Hanging out with family, having some fun. People weren't supposed to get sick, or become cruel, or change altogether. Layla wasn't sure how to make sense of what was going on around her.

Layla excused herself to go find the bathroom, needing a moment alone. Her cousin nodded nonchalantly, back on the phone, talking to her *beloved* Fareed. *Rah*.

'I'll wait here,' she mouthed to Layla.

Layla walked towards a bathroom sign, but there was no bathroom, only a cleaner's closet. Pursing her lips, she turned and started wandering around, immediately getting lost in the bustle and noise of the hospital. Trying to get her bearings, she took a deep, shuddering breath, her mind a jumble, and walked towards the brightest door she could see. Pushing it open, she stumbled out of the hospital and into the street.

This is definitely not the bathroom . . .

The noise and heat of the street assaulted her as she drifted into the bright afternoon sun. A loud din could be heard in the distance, the protests kicking on. *Rakshaat* beeped loudly, a donkey brayed in the distance and light sand caked everything as far as the eye could see.

Layla felt the urge to call Dina, or Ethan, or even Seb at this point (*though what he would say to me in reassurance I don't know*). She just wanted someone to tell her everything would be okay, help her understand what was going on, make everything right again. Between her grandmother in hospital, the case of the missing GDT member (her), Yousra having a *boyfriend*, and not knowing whether or not she was Sudaniya, this was *not* the halal girl summer she thought she was going to have.

CHAPTER 11

RUBBISH was scattered all around the hospital entry: empty glass bottles, plastic bags, bits of cardboard. *Are there no bins around?* Layla shuffled through it all and sat her dusty rear on a just-as-dusty bench outside the hospital doors. It had only been a day since they'd arrived in Sudan, but it already felt like an eternity. She swung her legs under the bench, brushing specks off her light brown skirt, and let her mind wander. She took in deep, soothing breaths to calm herself.

Oh. Wait. Layla's breath stopped in her throat.

'*Ya-nahr-aswad*,' Layla said out loud, uttering her favourite grandmother swearing phrase. She'd totally forgotten about sending the GDT minutes to the team!

Fishing her phone out of her pocket, Layla tried to see if there was a network she could connect to. *Nada.* No reception, no nearby unsecured wifi networks, no one around she felt like she could ask to hotspot from. Layla scrunched up her face, tired, frustrated and upset. Ya Allah, *you've really piled it on!* Her grandmother being sick, the argument with Yousra, these protests . . . and on top of all of that, trying to make sure Peter didn't suspect that she was out of the country and somehow hiding her involvement from Baba so she didn't get caught!

Layla let out a loud frustrated yell, startling a stray dog that had laid down gently in front of her.

Am I overreacting?

Maybe it was fine if she sent in the minutes from the meeting a few days late?

Hmmm. Peter isn't in a super-forgiving mood at the moment. LOL, when was Peter ever in a forgiving mood.

'Layla, are you okay?' Yousra had followed

her cousin outside and obviously seen Layla yell at . . . nobody.

Layla turned to look at Yousra, grimacing. It was best to pretend nothing was wrong. 'Oh Yous, hey!?'

'You didn't find the bathroom, I'm guessing?'

'Oh, yeh, nah . . .' Layla tried to sound positive. 'But I've got a bladder like Bolt,' she said, referring to the milkman's donkey.

Yousra frowned at her cousin with concern, but decided not to ask any more questions about the bathroom trip, or her cousin's strange sense of humour. 'Should we go get the snacks?' she said, changing the subject.

'Yeh . . .'

Yousra narrowed her eyes at her cousin. 'Layla, what's really going on? I can see you fiddling with your phone like you're some desperado. Tell me.'

Layla sucked in a gulp of air, deciding to take the plunge.

'*Habibi*, Yousra, do you know where I can find a hotspot right now? I need to send a message I totally forgot about.'

Yousra's green and gold flecked eyes gleamed with curiosity. 'Aha, so you do have a boy back home, ay?' her voice teased. 'Is this why you're so keen to get online?'

Layla shuddered at the idea of Peter being 'her boy'. '*La, la*, it's for the GDT, now *shhhh*!'

'The what?'

'Okay.' Layla's shoulder's slumped. 'Let me start from the top.'

Layla gave Yousra the run-down – how hard she'd worked to get a scholarship, the fact that she'd got suspended, the gummy bear invention, her role as secretary of the national championship GDT team and how she was selected for the prestigious spot on the SIIT.

'Okay, so you need to message them so they know you're working on the minutes and are going to send them very soon. Are you sure they wouldn't have noticed you're not in Australia any more?'

'Well, only Dina and my friends know,' Layla replied. 'Plus, if I send the minutes, how will they suspect anything?'

'And you haven't done that?'

Layla cleared her throat awkwardly. 'No. I finished them this morning, but I haven't found any internet yet.'

Yousra lips stretched flat against her teeth.

'Why not? You know we have wifi at home? Layla, you seem pretty terrible at sneaking around.'

'And what, you're the expert?' Although Layla was relieved to hear she could get wifi at the house, she was getting mildly frustrated by Yousra's know-it-all attitude. She was only one year older!

Yousra shrugged. 'I'm not saying that, but no one knows about Fareed, that's for sure.'

'Fine, whatever,' Layla huffed, trying to ignore Yousra's bragging and focus on the urgent task at hand. 'The thing is, cuz, I'm as stuffed as Habooba's *ma7shi* if I don't get these minutes sent off like, ASAP!'

'Okay, calm down. So, why don't you ask for a sim card from your mama or baba? I'm sure they won't mind.'

Layla dropped her head in her hands again.

'There's one more thing. Baba told me to quit the GDT team.'

Yousra scoffed and threw her hands up in the air. '*Ya bit!* You should have started with that! That's it then. There's no problem! Just clear it all up with your team when you're back or something. How were you meant to be a part of the team from here anyway?'

Layla raised her eyebrows at her cousin. *She really doesn't get it!*

'Yousra, listen. I can't just quit.'

'Why not? Your baba said you should, *mush khalas?*'

Layla's eyes widened, aghast at the suggestion she should listen to her dad's instruction to quit. 'No way. I just can't. This is the ticket to my future, *Inshallah*. Like, the international GDT is important, yes, but the Invention Tour? It means I get to travel the world, meeting the greatest inventors. It can help me find a scholarship at a fancy university, or maybe help me with a mentor or an internship. It's my ticket to the inventing future I have been praying for.'

Yousra's serene expression turned into one of genuine surprise, creasing her baked on foundation. 'Wow, okay, *habiba*. I didn't realise it was so important to you.' She checked her phone. 'I would help, but I've run out of data.'

'It's fine. I will handle it.'

Layla jumped to her feet. It was time to stop feeling sorry for herself and take matters into her own hands. She could fix things by herself, she always did. Maybe there was some secret hospital wifi that she could get onto? She waved at Yousra to stay put, then walked into the hospital reception to speak to the lady behind the counter.

'*Fi wai fai?*' she asked, querying about whether there was a wifi network she could access.

The woman staffing the reception looked even more bored than the lady at the airport had, but at Layla's request, she too cracked a disdainful smile.

'*Inti min wayn, ya bitana?*'

Layla sighed. *I am so over people wondering where I'm from.*

'*Ana min hina,*' she said in reply, indicating that she was from 'here'.

The aunty laughed throatily, the white *toub* rustling around her face and her henna-tipped fingers drumming on the desk in pleasure at the new plaything in front of her. '*Bilaaaahi?*' she continued in her Sudanese Arabic croon.

The aunty pursed her lips, the tribal markings on her face moving hypnotically as she changed expressions.

'Where are you living now?' The aunty switched into a heavily accented English, adding further insult to injury.

Rah, do I have to explain myself to every single person I meet?

Suppressing a deep sigh out of respect, Layla responded. 'I live in Australia, but I was born in Khartoum,' she replied, still speaking Arabic. Layla was going to show this lady that she was as Sudanese as the rest of them.

The woman's eyes glimmered; Layla felt about an inch tall under her gaze.

Focus, Layla. Don't let her aunty powers overwhelm you.

'*Almuhim ya ustazah, fi wai fai ana mumkin asta3mal?*' With that, Layla smirked internally. She had asked again about wifi, but in a voice dripping with so much sarcasm, Layla was surprised the counter between them hadn't got wet.

The receptionist's black eyebrow – only the left one – lifted up so high on her forehead it disappeared underneath her hairline. 'Young lady, this is not an internet cafe, this is a hospital. *MUSTASHFA*,' she sounded out the Arabic word for hospital loudly and slowly, as if Layla couldn't understand the language at all.

Exasperated and mildly humiliated, Layla considered walking away, but her desperation for internet was more pressing than her pride. Layla persisted. '*Low sama7ti, madam,*' she asked politely, changing tack. 'Where can I find an internet cafe nearby?'

The receptionist scoffed, leaning back in her chair. 'Do I look like Google maps to you?' she replied, then spun around to rustle through her handbag, effectively ending the conversation.

Layla slapped her forehead with her palm, growling. That was the most *unhelpful* conversation she'd ever had in her life! Turning, she saw Yousra approaching with a grin on her face.

'*Habiba*, come quickly! Habooba is awake!' said Yousra.

Habooba. This was why she was here. Everything else was less important. Habooba!

'*Alhamdulilah*, what a relief!'

'Yes, *Alhamdulilah*, and she's already started bossing the nurses and doctors around, so she must be feeling better.'

They smiled at each other and hugged, Layla feeling some of the tension between them from before melting away. But the relief was momentary, when a nagging returned to Layla.

'Yousra, what about a sim card?'

Yousra rolled her eyes dismissively. 'Layla, it can wait. We can get a sim and some data for me later. Come say hi to Habooba.'

Yousra pulled Layla's hand, dragging her back through the bustling hallways and into the room where the family was crowding around the newly awoken grandmother.

Layla smiled nervously as Yousra pulled her to Habooba's side. Layla kissed her grandmother's lined cheeks, trying to make her greetings heard among the loud prayers and shouting nurses around them. Soon though, the family's infectious energy caught on, and Layla felt herself relaxing into a big, toothy smile. She was so relieved Habooba was out of the woods. *Alhamdulilah!*

Feeling like she'd done enough greetings and prayers and cheek kissing, Layla wondered whether this meant the whole ordeal was over. If Habooba was well, did that mean Layla could get back to the GDT?

'Does this mean we can go back to Australia now?' Layla mused.

The twins, standing next to Layla, gasped, shocked at her brashness.

Fadia turned to her daughter, her face a dark storm.

Uh oh. I wasn't supposed to say that out loud.

CHAPTER 12

FADIA'S mouth twisted into an ominous scowl of anger and disappointment. Layla cowered instinctively, ready for the verbal lashing she was sure was coming. The air felt still and charged. Layla's mother narrowed her eyes, appearing to weigh up whether to tear her daughter to shreds for the insulting behaviour now, or later. Before she made a decision, Habooba interrupted from the bed.

'*Gulti shinu, ya bit?*' Habooba called out, teasingly asking what Layla had just said. 'You want to leave your grandmother already? What is this? You don't want to spend time with me, ah?

You only want me when I'm cooking nice things for you?' she chuckled, almost to herself.

Layla turned back to her grandmother, smiling bashfully.

Saved by Habooba!

'No, no, you know I love you in every way, ya Habooba,' Layla replied in Arabic, holding her grandmother's hand. 'The food is just a bonus, of course.'

Her grandmother's eyes, cloudy with cataracts, still managed to twinkle somehow. She smiled, her lips lifting up at the edges, like they were being pulled by fine string. *'Ta3ali hina, ya habiba.* I've missed you and you've grown so much! Tell me about what has been going on in your life.'

Layla rushed to her grandmother's side, excited to be able to talk to her about all the things that had happened since they'd last seen each other. She settled herself onto the edge of the bed, still holding her grandmother's rough and knobbly hand, and the twins gathered around.

'Okay, well,' Layla began, launching into a chronological history of the last five years.

Sami and Yousif acted as mini hype boys, adding sound effects as Layla regaled her grandmother with stories. When Layla got to the bit about the SIIT, Habooba Samira's eyelids dropped, and she started snoring. Layla looked over at her mum.

Did I literally bore her to sleep?

'Is she sleeping or is she –'

BANG!! BOOM!! BANG!!!

A series of deafening noises came from outside the building, reverberating through the hospital and interrupting Layla's question. She heard screaming, then sounds of breaking glass and people running. Layla started to breathe heavily, struggling to get air into her lungs. She stood up abruptly and tried to move, but her feet were rooted to the ground. The world closed in around her, and Layla found herself fading away . . .

'Layla! Layla! LAYLA!'

Layla opened her eyes carefully, straining a little where her eyelashes were stuck together. Eyes open, she was immediately blinded by bright white light.

Where am I?

She felt the cold, tiled floor underneath her and as she blinked, the world came into focus. Concerned faces peered down at her: Yousra, Mama, Sami and Yousif, a nurse.

'What happened?' she asked, as she tried to sit up. 'Is this heaven? Are we all in *jannah*?'

'*Shhh, shh, sh*,' her mother shushed her, pushing Layla's shoulders back down to the ground. 'This is not heaven. Sorry to disappoint you. Lie down, rest. You seem to have fainted and hit your head on the tiles. Someone has gone to get you some water and something to eat. Have you eaten anything today?'

Layla thought about the day: morning prayers, hanging out with Ma'ab on the patio, coming through the protests to the hospital, trying to look for internet – *internet! The GDT! Oh man I've REALLY got to get on that!* Her temple throbbed and she shook her head. 'No, I don't think I've eaten anything.'

'No wonder you're fainting, then, *ya habiba*. Why didn't you say anything? It's almost *asr*, and you must be tired and jet lagged.'

Layla wondered when everyone else had eaten. It must have been while she was working on changing the car engine oil with Ma'ab, after they had made all the protest posters. She'd never had the chance to work on a car before, so it was quite a lot of fun. But clearly, she'd missed out on brunch.

Rah, I can't believe I fainted.

The last time she was flat on her back on the ground was because of a fight she'd had on the first day of school. This was a lot less glamourous. Although, given the loud noises, it certainly had sounded like there had been a fight.

'What happened? I heard some bangs. Is Habooba okay?' Layla's voice was dry and raspy, every word painful to say. She tried to swallow, but couldn't. 'There were noises . . .'

'Habooba is fine, *Alhamdulilah*,' Fadia started to say, but Yousra was talking on top of her.

'The protestors were being shot at,' Yousra said at the same time.

Layla's eyes opened wide. *WHAT? That is HECTIC.*

Fadia saw her daughter's face seize up with anxiety again and quickly knelt down to rub her shoulders soothingly. 'Don't worry too much about it, *habiba*. It was just some soldiers not following orders. Everything is fine, it will all be over soon, everything is going to be all right. I'm sure Ozzie and the boys are safe too, *Inshallah*.' Though her words were reassuring, it sounded like she was trying convince herself more than Layla.

Everything was not fine! Her stomach curdling slightly, Layla refocused on the room around her, the faces of her siblings coming in and out of focus. The twins looked terrified and Yousra wore a mask of concern.

I can get up, no worries. Habooba is the really sick one here.

As she tried to push herself off the ground one more time, a sharp pain ricocheted around her skull, like a ping-pong fireball.

Ahhhhh!

Layla lay back on the ground.

'I'm just going to stay down here for now.'

Yousra nodded soothingly, and gently rubbed Layla's head. 'Relaaaax, *habiba*.'

CHAPTER 13

LATER that evening, back at the house, Layla sat at the dinner table. It felt safe and familiar, a relief after so many new and unfamiliar experiences. The table creaked with delicious food (including *aseeda*!) and family: Yousra, Ma'ab and Mohammed, Ozzie, Sami and Yousif, Baba, Khalu Marwan and Amal. Mama was still at the hospital with Habooba.

Amal was a quiet, round woman with light skin and rosy cheeks, who always spoke incredibly softly, as if she was soothing a sleeping baby. She was a masterclass in homely Sudanese hospitality, fussing around Layla, Sami and Yousif, making sure they were all fed and watered, filling their glasses with guava juice and chatting to them in cool, calm tones. Sami and Yousif had been quite rattled by the events of the afternoon and were uncharacteristically quiet all evening. Ma'ab, Mohammed and Ozzie had just got in from the protests, their faces flush with energy and adrenalin.

'I hope you weren't planning on flying out any time soon,' said Khalu Marwan to Baba, as he spooned some *mulaa7* and *aseeda* into his mouth.

'Why?' asked Layla, her ears perking up.

'The government shut down the airport,' Ma'ab helpfully added.

'You're stuck with us for now,' Mohammed said, grinning mischievously.

Sami and Yousif looked at each other, then Layla, then their father, bottom lips trembling.

'You mean, forever?' asked Yousif.

Mohammed nodded, eyes open super wide for effect. 'You . . . will . . . never . . . LEAVE!' he teased.

The younger twins jumped in their seats, yelping and starting to cry.

Layla shushed them. 'He's lying, it's not true.'
Was it? She had no idea.

'Don't worry, you can keep busy by working
with me on the generator,' Ma'ab smiled at Layla.

Layla simpered awkwardly. Although that did
sound like fun, she really needed to get back to
the GDT team. Also, she *still* hadn't emailed the
team the minutes!

'That's enough now, *yallah*,' said Khaltu Amal,
bringing some order back to the table.

'But wait, is it true, *ya Khaltu*?' Layla asked.
Wombats couldn't fly themselves back to Australia, you see. This was going to be a problem.

Amal took in a deep breath. 'We don't know,
ya Layla. We just don't know.'

Straight after dinner, they all piled up in front of
the TV, watching the news about the protests.
Sami and Yousif were dozing off.

'So, do you still want to use the wifi, Layla ya
Lazeeza?' Yousra asked, her voice teasing. Yousra
called her by the nickname only her family in Sudan
used, a nickname Layla hadn't heard in a while.

Layla nodded but without enthusiasm, still a little irritated. Layla didn't know if she could sit through another lecture about her lack of Sudaniness or her no-boyfriend status. These were things that seemed to make even less sense now that she'd had some time to think about it. How was it that in Australia at ISB people told them it was *haram* to have boyfriends, but in Sudan, where the majority of people were Muslim, her cousins had them? Layla wondered whether maybe 'boyfriend' – or *jiks* – meant a different type of thing in Sudan than it did in Brisbane.

'Yes! But can I *please* have the password without another long story about my non-existent *jiks*, okay? It's done.'

Yousra laughed and rolled her eyes. 'You're too serious, Layla, *wallahi*. Just calm down, *mafi mushkilla*. Everything will be fine.'

'*Inshallah*,' Layla added under her breath.

Yousra started to giggle, her laugh – even when laughing at Layla – somehow still glorious, like Christmas bells in a Disney movie.

If I was pretty like Yousra, everything would be fine. Maybe that's why Yousra has a jiks *and I don't.*

Kissing her teeth, Layla chided herself for the thought. It was no use comparing herself to Yousra like that. They were family after all. Plus, she might not look like the girls on TV, but she had her own fabulous features, like her strong muscles and creative brain. Also, all of this chatter was valuable time away from the internet, and Yousra held the key. Thank goodness Khalu Marwan had a wifi dongle!

Password in hand, Layla walked out of the TV area to connect her phone. As soon as there was a whiff of signal, Layla's phone immediately began having conniptions with the number of messages coming through all at once. The handset had not been on silent either, so the buzzing, beeping, pinging and tinging made it seem like the phone itself would need to be checked into the hospital.

'Wow, gurl, whoever he is, he really missed you,' Yousra teased.

Notifications from iMessage, WhatsApp, Snap, TikTok, Insta and every other social media platform were coming through, thick and fast. Layla noticed that the more recent ones started to include shouty capital letters. *Ya Allah*. Layla's stomach tied itself into knots as she prepared to wade through the barrage.

Just as she was about to open the first message, her phone rang. Layla's favourite Cardi B song started playing. The very non-halal lyrics filled the room. Layla stared at the caller ID.

It was Peter.

Peter? It was the middle of the night in Australia, what was he doing calling her now?

Do I pick up? For the second time that day, Layla froze.

As the mobile continued to ring, Yousra looked at her cousin, then at the phone. 'Ooooohhh, who is Peter? You naughty girl. You told me you didn't have a *jiks*, but I KNEW it! Layla is in looooove,' Yousra laughed.

Before Layla could react, Yousra grabbed the phone out of her palm and answered, putting it on speaker phone.

'Heyyyyy, baby,' she crooned into the mic, her Sudani English coated in velvet. 'I missed you. Have you missed me, Beter?'

The voice on the other end of the phone spluttered in confusion. 'Cut it out, Layla. What are you doing?' Peter's gruff Australian accent was tinny and jarring. 'Where the hell are ya?' He sounded extra annoyed.

'Uh,' Layla started, as she attempted to wrestle the phone out of Yousra's hands, but he interrupted her.

'You haven't answered any messages, and all your accounts say you've been offline for days! What the hell, man? Have you skipped town or something, you stupid terrorist?'

At the last comment, Yousra's playful expression dropped. She put the phone on mute, her face a mix of confusion and anger. 'Who is this guy and why is he talking to you like that?' she asked her cousin, horrified.

Layla didn't know whether to say to Yousra that Peter didn't really mean it, or to tell Peter off for being so rude and racist. First, she needed to make sure she stayed on the team, and that meant reassuring him that everything was fine (even though it wasn't!). Layla scrambled towards Yousra again to grab the phone from her. Peter was still speaking.

'Oi, answer me! What's going on, you mutt?'

Layla's heart sunk. She'd thought she was past this with Peter, thought they were on pretty good terms, thought that they could work together on the GDT without his racist bullying coming through once more. But it seemed like whenever he got really angry, he became the worst version of himself, hurting anyone within reach. *And then I have to deal with the fallout!*

Finally grabbing the phone back from Yousra, Layla pressed unmute. 'Peter, mate, calm down,' Layla said into the phone. 'And chill with the names, okay? That was just my cousin, Yousra. She thinks I have a boyfriend, and thought that *we* had something going on, that's why she answered the phone like that. Mate, it was a joke.' Layla's face burned with embarrassment and she gave Yousra a glaring side-eye that would make Beyoncé proud.

Yousra mouthed 'sorry!' in Arabic back at her cousin, though her face still wore a scowl.

'Something going on, yeh right,' Peter scoffed. 'If by something going on, you mean you getting kicked off the team?'

Layla's heart dropped even further, swimming with the fishes of the deep sea. This was exactly what she was afraid of.

'What are you talking about, Peter?' she asked

carefully. 'I'm here man, I'm here. I'm with ya, I'm fully involved –'

He scoffed again. 'You're not here at all! You were supposed to have sent a sketch for our invention idea already, but we haven't heard a thing from you. You're supposed to be the creative, mechanical brain. Why weren't you at the meeting today?'

Layla sucked in her breath. *There was a meeting today?! Oh no!* Layla had thought it was tomorrow, but that was before all the time zone differences. *Janey MACK!* She wasn't doing anything right.

'Dude, my grandmother got super sick. We're visiting her in the hospital. I've just been so busy with everything I haven't checked my phone. You know how it is.' Layla prayed he would accept her explanation.

'Look, whatever about your grandmother, but you can't just disappear on us. There's a lot of work to be done on this project, you know that, and we need everyone to be fully present so that we can *win* this thing!' Peter's voice rose to a yell by the end of the sentence. 'So, see you at the next meeting then? You'll need to get the agenda sorted tonight. And send those minutes through. I want them in my inbox before I wake up.'

Layla gulped. This was tricky. She needed to convince Peter not to kick her off the team, but she also wasn't sure when she would be back. *Bah!* When would they reopen the airport, when there was a new government? People had been talking about a new government since Layla was born. It wasn't likely to happen any time soon. How was she going to balance this?

'Oi!' Peter's voice jolted Layla out of her reflections.

Without thinking, Layla replied. 'Yeh, yup, yeh, I'll be there, and if I can't leave the hospital, I'll call in from the ward. I'll make sure all the paperwork is sent over as well. Before you wake up. It'll all be fine, okay?'

Peter huffed his displeasure over the phone. 'Fine. I'm holding ya to that.'

'Oh, that's great. Thanks, Peter.'

'But if you miss one more meeting without notice, that's it, you're out of the team.'

'Huh? Why? I thought it was if I missed three meetings in a –'

The phone line went dead.

'*YA-NAHR-ASWAD!*' Layla yelled at the phone, startling Yousra.

'*Habiba*, was that guy your boyfriend?' Yousra asked. 'He sounded . . . umm . . . I'm not sure how I feel about him calling you a terrorist. Is that some Australian flirting technique?'

'Oh, Yousra, no! He's Peter, the head of the GDT, the guy I headbutted, remember? I told you the story.'

'OMG, that's the guy?' Yousra's eyes almost fell out of her head in shock.

Layla continued. 'He's not my boyfriend, he's the worst bully in the world!'

As the enormity of the situation dawned on her, tears sprung to Layla's eyes. 'I need to be at that meeting otherwise they'll kick me out of the group and then I can't go to the international GDT, and I've been working on it all year, and the worst thing is –' deep breath '– I'm scared that if I fail, Mr Cox will kick me out of school permanently this time.'

'*Habiba*, I'm so sorry. I had no idea *that* was the guy you were telling me about. Don't worry, we will figure something out, right?' Yousra's tune had changed completely, as she kneeled and rubbed her bawling cousin's back, softly, sooth-ingly. 'Don't worry, *habiba*, don't worry.'

'Figure what out, exactly, ya Yousra?'

Both Yousra and Layla froze, as they heard a deep voice behind them.

It was Baba. And he did *not* look impressed.

CHAPTER 14

OH NO!

Layla swallowed, pressing her lips tightly together to stop the sound of her crying. A high-pitched whimper escaped, and Yousra squeezed Layla's arm in warning.

'What is it that you are crying about, ya Layla?'

Kareem was usually the nicer parent. Fadia was the one who did the disciplining. What that meant was if Kareem *did* get angry, it was really not a good time.

Layla gulped, hurriedly wiping her tears away. 'Oh, nothing, Baba. Seriously . . .'

'Nothing? It doesn't feel like nothing to me. Are you having boy troubles? I heard something about a boyfriend.'

He heard something about a boyfriend?!

How long had he been standing there, listening? Layla's heart skipped a beat, but she could handle this. If she could handle Peter and Chairman Cox, she could handle anyone, right?

'No, Baba. Of course I don't have boy troubles. I would never do such a thing, you know me.'

Kareem nodded slowly, the ends of his lips pulling downward. 'Okay, no boy troubles. That's good, that's good.' He paused. 'There's nothing else?'

Layla shook her head, vehemently and silently communicating to her cousin. *He can't know about the GDT. He told me I'm not allowed to be in it any more, so I don't know what he'll do!*

Kareem looked at the girls musingly, putting his hands in his pockets, then turned to walk away. Yousra and Layla stole a glance at each other, relief etched on their faces as they realised they had got away with it.

But just as he was taking a step, Kareem turned back. 'So, then, I must have been imagining things when I heard you talking about the GDT to Peter Cox?'

Layla's stomach dropped right into the earth's mantle.

Janey Mack. She was *busted*.

Yousra and Layla sat forlornly on the couch in front of the TV. Kareem had unceremoniously shushed everyone else out of the room, so Layla knew that they were really going to get it.

Ya Allah. *How do I get out of this one?*

'Listen, Baba, it isn't what you think –' Layla started, but Baba silenced her with a single glare.

'No, Layla, you need to listen.'

Yousra sat incredibly still next to Layla, staring straight ahead. Kareem paced up and down the room, like a lion in a cage, clearly wanting to pounce, but too careful a man to do so. He eventually slowed to a stop in the middle of the room and looked at the girls. Layla tried to swallow, but her throat was as parched as the Sahara Desert.

'Yousra, what do you know about this?' Kareem asked.

'About what, *Khalu*?'

'About the GDT competition?'

Yousra shook her head, implying that she knew nothing . . . or that she was going to say nothing. Layla internally rejoiced: at least her cousin wasn't going to throw her under the bus.

'Layla.' Kareem turned to his daughter.

Her mouth was still so dry. 'Yes, Baba?' she rasped.

'What do you have to say for yourself?'

Layla's mind scrambled. What excuse did she have for disobeying her dad?

'I don't know, Baba. It's just . . .' Layla cleared her throat. This was her only chance to get her father back on side. 'I worked so so sooo hard to get selected for the Special International Invention Tour. It's kind of a big deal. I couldn't just give it up! Also, the GDT team is depending on me to come up with something amazing to take to Germany.'

'And what about what I said? Why did you continue doing GDT work when I told you to stop?'

For a split second, Layla considered making something up, some story that would be more convincing. But alas, she knew she was a terrible liar . . . *and it's the wrong thing to do!*

'Well, I thought maybe if I continued doing GDT stuff and it wasn't disruptive, then you could see that there would be no need for me to quit.' Layla really hoped she was making a good enough case to convince her father. 'I don't want to accept just anything, Baba. I don't want to end up like –' Layla paused. She didn't want to end up being miserable like Ozzie, doing a job he hated. But was saying that one step too far? 'I really want to do this.'

'So, you disobeyed me because you thought you knew better?' Kareem's tone was slow, sure, calm.

Janey Mack. It was a trap! *Abort mission, abort mission!*

'Oh no, Baba, that's not what I meant at all!'

Layla shot a look at Yousra, a silent klaxon for backup, but her cousin was fastidiously studying her nails.

'Sounds to me, ya Layla, like you do whatever it is you *want* to do, without thinking at all about how it impacts the people around you,' said Baba. 'Does that sound about right?'

No!

'No, that's not fair at all!'

'Oh, really? So, when your grandmother is sick in hospital, your mother is with her and your aunts and uncles are running around making sure you're all taken care of, your main focus is on your invention competition so that *you* can go to Germany? So that *you* can go on your *Special International Invention Tour*, like some princess in a fairytale. Have you thought that maybe all of us are giving things up? Have you thought about helping your mother, asking what she needs? Have you thought about asking your aunty if she needs help? Have you thought about *anyone* other than yourself in this situation?'

Now Layla was annoyed. Kareem hadn't had a go at anyone else, and it wasn't like she was the only one not helping.

'Baba, this is *so* unfair! You don't ask Ozzie whether he's helping. Why are you blaming me? Ozzie straight up ignored Mama's instructions when he went to the protest this morning, and he didn't even get in trouble. Why am I always the one who gets in trouble? Why are you –'

'Because you are acting selfish, ya Layla. You do not *listen*!' Kareem interrupted, his anger boiling over. 'Layla, *khalas*, that's it.' Kareem took in a deep breath and removed his glasses, rubbing his face with the free hand. 'You're grounded.'

'What?!' said Layla and Yousra simultaneously.

'You heard me, Layla. You're grounded.'

'No! No, Baba, please!'

'*Khalas*. Habooba is coming home soon, *Inshallah*. You're to stay with her and help with anything she needs. No going outside, no visiting cousins, no popping to the shops, nothing. Maybe Habooba can teach you how to listen a little better.'

'But *Khalu*!' pleaded Yousra.

Layla was so thankful Yousra was with her on this.

'But nothing,' Kareem replied. 'And, Yousra, you're lucky I'm not grounding you too,' he sighed.

On that note, Layla's dad left the room.

'Oh man!' Layla cried, as soon as her father left.

'*Habiba*, that's so bad,' Yousra replied, grimacing.

'I'm gonna have to be extra sneaky about calling into team meetings now.'

Yousra looked at Layla, nonplussed. 'You're still thinking about that invention competition?'

Layla nodded, trying to keep it together.

'Maybe your dad's right, you're too obsessed!' said Yousra.

Layla scoffed. 'Oh yeh? Not as obsessed as you are with Fareed.'

Yousra opened her mouth in mock shock and threw a pillow at Layla.

'*Askuti, ya bit!*'

They both laughed.

Well, at least I'm stuck inside with one of my favourite cousins.

That night after *3isha* prayers, Layla prayed two extra *rak3aat* for her grandmother's health, two for the protesters and two to get her out of being grounded. *I'm sure you're already quite busy, ya Allah, working on sorting out malaria and mad cow disease and Palestine, but if you could give us a hand here, that would be the absolute best. Please, please, please? I will even be extra nice to Peter, just for you.* Shukran.

Layla woke with a start, again. *Dasted jet lag!* The sun still hadn't come up, but there was no way she was falling back to sleep now. She turned and twisted, getting tangled in the thin sheets and her cotton *jalabeeya*, before deciding to get up and start the day.

Brush teeth, pray *fajr*, check phone. Do some secret GDT work. Layla nodded to herself, planning her morning. *Let's see how Dina is . . .* Layla had figured out that she could stay connected to Khalu Marwan's wifi. She had sent the minutes to the GDT team last night, and now she could message her friend.

Layla
D!!! I miss you so much. Things are so hectic here.

Dina
Yeh, must b intense. Ur granma ok?

Layla
She woke up yesterday, Al7, bt duno. Shes sposd 2b cmin home sn.

Dina
Al7. Does that mean ur bk sn or . . .?

Layla

Inshallah ay. But yo the GDT stuff is so wild.

Dina

Wym?

Layla

Peter sd hed kick me out if I didn cum 2danxt meeting. But Baba has said I can't be in the group any more . . . so yeh.

Dina

Urgh. Sis.

Layla

That's not helpful, D!

Dina

Lol ur kinda screwed, L.

In that moment, Layla didn't feel remotely like a queen or even a regular teen. She felt like an insignificant insect; a little ant, or a fly, lost in a new neighbourhood, wandering around with no direction. As she closed her eyes, a single tear rolled down her cheek. Her emotions were on a constant roller-coaster in Sudan. *Oh Allah, have mercy . . .*

Exhaling loudly, Layla wiped the tear dry and decided to go for a wander around the house to get some inspiration for the GDT. Peter wanted her to come up with some new creative ways they could 'level up' their robot, and Layla had *nothing* at the moment. Feeling like there was too much going on wasn't exactly the recipe for a brilliant idea, so maybe an early morning walk would help. Softly, quietly, so as not to wake anyone, she stepped outside to the back area of the house. This area was quiet, unused, dust-caked tiles and crusty mops. There was a shed, a clothes-line . . . Layla started roaming around the back patio, lost in thought.

'Layla, what are you doing up?' said a voice out of nowhere.

Huh?!

'Who is that?'

Someone was whispering from the back shed Layla had just walked past.

Layla turned back to the shed. She pushed the door, peering into the darkness. 'Ma'ab? Why are *you* up so early?'

Ma'ab, down on his haunches, sighed. 'It's the only way I can work on this in peace.'

Layla stepped further into the cramped space. 'What are you working on?' Her curiosity was piqued.

'It's the diesel generator I was telling you about. I found it on the street a few months ago. It's pretty broken, but I reckon we can get it going again.'

'Why do you need a generator?' Layla asked. It seemed like a cool project, but a little random.

Ma'ab chuckled. 'Oh, you *khawajaat* don't know what it's like, do you?'

Layla rolled her eyes. 'I'm not a foreigner!'

'No, seriously, ya Layla. During summer, we have no electricity for, like, ten hours a day sometimes. Do you know how hot it gets? It's, like, over fifty degrees. We need electricity for the fridge, the fans, the aircoolers – a diesel generator can help us when the electricity cuts out.'

Layla's eyes widened. 'Why is there no electricity like that?'

Ma'ab sighed. 'Oh, I dunno.' He rubbed his head hard, the short curly hair barely moving underneath his fingers. 'It's what happens when the government stops functioning properly, you know? They spend money on themselves instead of basic services for the people, like electricity, water or rubbish collection.'

'Oh.' Layla looked around, as if to remember what it was like outside the house. 'Is that why there is always rubbish everywhere?'

Ma'ab nodded. 'In Brisbane, where you live, where does the rubbish go?'

Layla frowned as she recalled. 'Well, we put it in wheelie bins, then a rubbish truck comes once a week and takes it to, I dunno, the dump or something?'

'And what would happen if the rubbish truck didn't come one week?' Ma'ab continued.

Layla scowled. 'Oh, that would be so gross. The streets would start to stink probably.'

'Now, imagine if all the rubbish drivers just quit, because they weren't getting paid at all.'

Layla fell quiet. 'Is that what's happening?'

Ma'ab softly bowed his head. 'Yeh. That's what's happening. The country is falling apart, and it's not our fault, and it's just not fair. And we young people are stuck with it. It's these fools in power, the ones sitting at the top who don't care about us little ones on the street. *But!*' Ma'ab straightened up. 'That's why we fight for justice, Layla.'

'Is there no other way, other than fighting?'

'What do you think?'

Layla had so many thoughts and questions, but before she could say another word, Ma'ab's phone rang, distracting him.

'Oh, I gotta get this, Layla,' he said. 'It's about the protests. We can finish this later, okay?'

Layla nodded. She finally understood (mostly) what was going on. *Wow.* She realised how proud she felt of her cousin, fighting to make his country better. Layla wondered if she should be doing something similar. In Sudan or Australia . . . or both? If she was Sudaniya, did that mean she should get involved in the fight for a better future too?

Ya Allah, *please help Sudan!*

Casting her eyes around the shed and thinking about the conversation with Ma'ab had given her an idea though.

Finally, I can send something to Peter to keep him happy.

Using the notes app on her phone, she drew in a couple of sketches, with a few dot points to explain the idea and sent it off to the team.

Bismillah!

CHAPTER 15

A few hours later, the rest of Habooba's house was up and about. Yousra, in a bid to get her cousin to forget about being grounded, pretended nothing had happened. Layla felt relieved and thankful for her generosity. They swapped clothes and stories, Yousra sharing tidbits about her past boy entanglements (*so many!*) and Layla describing what life was like at her new school. Her cousin was curious about what the *khawajaat* at Layla's new school were actually like.

'Do they eat pork all the time?' Yousra asked.

'Yeh, lol. They really love bacon.'

Yousra screwed up her nose. 'So weird. What about, does everyone have a boyfriend or girlfriend?'

Layla thought about it. 'I feel like everyone *wants* a boyfriend or girlfriend or *jiks*, but not everyone gets one.'

Yousra nodded. 'Same as here, then.'

Layla raised her eyebrows. 'Didn't you say everyone has a boyfriend?'

Yousra smiled slyly. 'Well, you know. Everyone who can get one, has one. I'm one of the lucky ones I guess.'

Layla shook her head. Of course Yousra was lucky. *Never did I think this is what Khartoum and Brisbane would have in common. Some girls just had 'it'.* Dina was like Yousra in that way too, 'lucky'. All the cute boys at the mosque wanted to follow her on Insta. *Sigh.*

Yousra held up her phone. 'Oh, Layla, come see this.'

She showed her cousin a flurry of protest videos from WhatsApp. Layla watched the scenes on the phone in awe. People, who looked just like her and her family, out on the streets, yelling for freedom and justice. She'd never seen anything like it before.

Subhanallah. Was this what revolution felt like?

Breakfast was loud and rowdy, and although the absence of Habooba Samira at the head of the table was glaringly obvious, the fact that she was now awake meant that they could talk about her without fear.

'Guess what, *ya shabab*? Habooba will hopefully be back today,' Khalu Marwan announced.

Cheers erupted around the table.

Alhamdulilah! *At least one thing was going right.*

Fadia had stayed with Habooba at the hospital last night and Kareem was at his sister's house across town. Even though the parents were out, Layla felt like she was at home. One of the best parts of being in Sudan was that you could find that feeling in so many different houses.

'I gotta get ready for school,' Yousra announced, getting up from the table. Just as she was leaving, the radio and TV news announced that all schools and universities were closed for the rest of the week because of the civil unrest. Layla was thrilled that they could spend all day together now.

As breakfast was being cleared up, Ma'ab, Mohammed and Ozzie announced that they were going to visit the gathering at the front of the military headquarters. Apparently the sit-in had become a festival of sorts. And some of the twins' friends had been sleeping there for almost a week.

'I don't know about that. The army are getting a bit dangerous,' Marwan mused, and Amal softly agreed.

'Nah, *mafi mushkilla*,' the older twins reassured their father.

'No one got injured yesterday,' Ma'ab said, confidently. 'The army was just flexing to scare people off protesting, but it's not going to work. The soldiers are pretty much on our side now, anyway.'

Khalu Marwan nodded his head slowly and begrudgingly acquiesced. 'Okay, you can go, but stay safe and keep us posted with where you are and your movements, okay? And make sure you come back home before the sun goes down.'

Layla saw her chance. She knew she was grounded, but surely they would let her out for this? Layla had decided it was time she got involved. She'd made posters, she'd told Yousra she was Sudaniya and she had been inspired by Ma'ab's passion. Even though she didn't fully know what freedom and justice meant, they felt important enough to fight for.

'Can I go too?' she asked her uncle. 'Please, please, please, *ya Khalu*. I will be safe with the boys; they will take care of me.' Layla was banking on the fact that Kareem hadn't told his brother-in-law about grounding her.

Marwan still didn't seem sure, but then the younger twins got involved. 'No, Layla, don't go,' they chimed together.

'Plus, Baba said you were to be ground.' Yousif added.

'*Shhh!*' Layla hushed the twins. *They're gonna rat me out!*

Sami and Yousif frowned at Layla, fear causing their bottom lips to tremble.

'The bangs were very loud yesterday,' Sami muttered.

Yousif nodded. 'Lots of scary noises and bad people . . .'

As they talked, the boys drew in around Layla, grabbing hold of her hands tightly. 'Stay here with us.'

'No, *ya shabab*. It's okay,' Layla reassured her little brothers.

Layla continued to plead with her uncle. 'Aw, c'mon, it's my Sudan too!'

That was the right thing to say for her elder cousins. Ma'ab piped up in her defence. 'Yeh, you know, ya Baba, she's right. It's her Sudan too, and she did help build the posters.'

'*7ureya, salam wa 3adala! Madaneeya khiyar alsha3b!*' Layla started chanting one of the main freedom chants she'd seen in the protest videos that morning. *Freedom, peace and justice. Civilian rule is the choice of the people!*

Marwan smiled in slight surprise at his Australian-bred niece's insistence on being involved in the Sudanese plight for freedom.

'*7ureya, salam wa 3adala! Madaneeya khiyar alsha3b!*' Layla chanted again, banging her fist on the table in time with the words. '*Yallah*, everybody!' and soon, the entire table was chanting.

'*7ureya, salam wa 3adala! Madaneeya khiyar alsha3b! 7ureya, salam wa 3adala! Madaneeya khiyar alsha3b! MADANEEEYYYAAAA.*'

The house reverberated with the passion of young people who wanted to see and build a better future. *Freedom, peace and justice! Civilian rule is the choice of the people!*

Layla could feel the energy rising around her, feel the passion of her cousins and family for freedom.

'What's all that noise?' a firm voice called, puncturing the mood.

Oh no.

Baba had just arrived, and with that, any hope of Layla leaving the house flew out the window.

The chanting stopped, and everyone turned to look at Kareem, who was walking through the mosquito net covering the front door.

'*Sabah alkhair*, Kareem,' Marwan called warmly.

'Nice chanting. I hope Layla has told you she's grounded and not allowed to leave the house.'

Khalu Marwan turned to Layla, eyebrow arched.

'Oh . . . yeh. That slipped my mind. I thought it was a bad dream.'

There was no getting out of this one! But luckily, there was some bigger news to deal with.

'Anyway, guess who I brought with me?'

Behind Kareem were two figures. Mama . . . and Habooba!

'Where are my rascal grandkids, ay?' Habooba called, and they all ran towards her, showering the elderly woman with love and tears of joy.

Later, while everyone was distracted, Layla snuck into the back shed and called into the GDT meeting. Alhamdulilah *Khalu's wifi works out here!* The signal was weak, but it worked.

Peter was being his annoying self. 'Layla, when are you going to be able to leave the hospital and join us in *person* at the meetings?' He asked over the call, a fountain of sarcasm and mistrust.

Layla grimaced. She still hadn't come clean about the fact that, well, she wasn't even in the same hemisphere and she had no idea when she would be back.

Why hadn't she said anything yet? Deep down, she knew.

The moment I say anything, it's all over!

Layla was sure if Peter somehow found out that she had skipped town without telling the team, she would be kicked out within the blink of an eye! It would make no difference that she didn't have a choice in the matter, or that it was because she had a sick grandmother, or that there was a revolution literally happening on her doorstep. None of that would change a thing.

At least he couldn't say she hadn't been doing her work though.

'Ahem! Anyone there?' Peter's voice startled Layla out of her thoughts again. 'So, are you going to be with us at the next meeting?'

'Oh, I dunno. I'm really worried about my grandma. Depends on how she's going, I guess.' Layla replied, laying the concern on thickly. Habooba was really settling in fine back at home, but Peter didn't need to know that. 'Do you want to talk to my mum about it or something?'

'Nah, nah, nah. Fine. Well, as long as you keep up with your work. I'm not a fan of any of these new ideas you've sent through at the moment, so we're going to need to keep brainstorming. *Quickly!*'

Layla breathed a sigh of relief. It was annoying that he hadn't liked any of the new ideas, but she was glad to have found a way to make him back off: suggesting Peter talk to Mama was the most effective method yet. The rest of the team didn't seem to mind much, although Layla occasionally got a text message from Penny asking where she was and why Layla was leaving her to fend for herself with all the boys. 'You'll be right!' Layla would voice note back, chuckling.

'Yeh, I was actually thinking of another idea. You might like this one –'

'Layla?' A banging came from the shed door.

Ya-nahr-aswad. *No, I can't get busted* again!

'Oh, hey, sorry guys. Something's up with my grandma. One sec.' Layla ended the call swiftly, tucked the phone behind a pot on a shelf, before jumping up to open the door.

Kareem walked in, hands clasped behind his back, inspecting the surroundings. The back shed was full of bric-a-brac and dust, old bits and pieces from machines and broken toys and used pots and furniture. Layla had thought it was a treasure trove when Ma'ab first showed it to her. Now, however, it felt too small for her, Kareem and his growing suspicion.

'Who were you talking to?' Kareem asked, slowly and deliberately.

'No one, just myself. You know, I like to talk to myself.'

'Hmm.' Kareem started walking around the shed, inspecting things. 'What's this?' he asked, pointing at Ma'ab's diesel generator.

'It's something Ma'ab is working on that he wanted my help with.'

'What does it do?'

'It's a generator – for electricity in summer.'

Kareem nodded, his index finger pushing his glasses up the bridge of his nose. The shed was quiet, sounds from outside muffled. And just as Kareem moved to leave the shed . . .

'Layla, where did you go, mate? Your GDT team is *waiting*,' Peter's voice rang out from her phone.

Kareem turned around to glare at Layla, eyebrows raised.

Raaaah!!! I thought I ended the call. How come it's now on speaker?!

'Where is your phone?' Kareem demanded.

Layla shook her head. This couldn't get any worse!

'Give me your phone. I'm confiscating it.'

'No!' Layla moved to the spot where the phone was hidden, trying to stop her dad from getting it. 'No, Baba, please!'

'Layla?' Penny's voice rang out, and Kareem's eyes narrowed.

'Give me your phone.'

Kareem stood in front of her, stern expression, hand outstretched. The silence drew longer.

Eventually Layla's shoulders slumped and she fished out the phone from its hiding place, handing it to her father.

This is a human rights violation!!!

Kareem switched to the call and put on his stern-but-kind voice. 'Hello there, students. Thanks so much for keeping Layla involved in the GDT, but I regret to inform you that she will no longer be participating in this competition. Her grandmother is very sick and it's important that Layla is focused and present for her grandmother's recovery.'

'Wait, what are you saying?' asked Peter, his voice confused.

'Layla is no longer a team member of the GDT. Okay, we need to go now. Bye.' Kareem ended the call, pocketed the phone and walked out of the shed.

Layla slowly sunk to her knees.

What. Just. Happened?!

CHAPTER 16

'YA Layla. Are you running around making a nuisance of yourself?' Habooba Samira called from the kitchen.

Habooba had barely rested after returning from the hospital, even though that was exactly what the doctor ordered. She had gone straight back to her regular routine, shutting down anyone who argued with her. 'If I'm going to just sit quietly and do nothing, what's the point of being alive?' she would say to her children who were constantly fussing about her.

Layla felt like she understood that. She never

really wanted to rest, because life was too short, right?

'Layla, come in here if you've got nothing else to do,' said Habooba.

Ah, damn, I'm gonna get chores now!

Habooba never passed up a chance to give one of the kids something to do, something to keep them occupied. Today, it seemed, was no exception.

'Habooba, I'm doing some homework,' Layla called from the bedroom, trying to see if she could talk her way out of getting chores. She was still reeling from Baba's phone confiscation and had thrown herself back into bed, moping and feeling sorry for herself.

'*Bilahi*?' Habooba called again. 'I thought you were on school holidays?'

Oh, I've definitely *been busted . . .*

Layla grinned to herself ruefully before dutifully trudging to the kitchen where her grandmother was standing in front of the gas stove. Habooba Samira wore a thinning pastel pink *jalabeeya* tied back with a worn brown apron, her greying hair pulled into a single long plait almost down to her thighs. Her hands, knotty with age, were working their magic over a pot so overflowing with smells it instantly made Layla weak at the knees.

'Oh, Habooba. What are you making?' Layla rushed to the side of the stove to peer into the pot, but her grandmother shushed her out of the way.

'Uh-uh! You'll burn yourself, *ya bit*,' Habooba Samira gently scolded her granddaughter.

Layla moved aside, but only slightly, craning her neck to get a good look. She inhaled deeply, taking in the spices: cumin, cardamom, pepper.

'Ouch!' Layla's neck snapped back as the steam from the pot burnt her nose and face.

Habooba lightly slapped her wrist. 'Didn't I tell you that you would burn yourself? Go wash your face with cold water, *yallah*.'

Sometimes Layla's curiosity did really get the better of her, she thought, as she washed her face with cool water to ease the burning.

'Okay, ya Habooba. If you don't want my face in the pot, what can I do to help?'

Habooba indicated to the small table in the centre of the crowded kitchen, a low tableau with an even smaller stool underneath it. On the table was a steel bowl full of vegetables – including tomatoes, cucumbers, capsicum, onion, carrots – with a chopping board and sharp knife placed next to it.

'You're going to help with the salad for lunch. *Yallah*, start cutting the vegetables up, and when you're done with that you can peel the potatoes for the stew.'

Layla groaned internally as she pulled the stool out and crouched down on the weaved seat. *I always do the unimportant things like chopping and peeling.*

'Are you going to call Ozzie to help too?' she asked. At least if they were doing it together, Layla could make fun of him.

Habooba chuckled. 'Of course not. The kitchen isn't for boys. Ozzie will help outside with the men.' She rolled her eyes dramatically. 'Imagine! Ozzie in the kitchen! What would people say?'

Layla screwed up her nose, irritated. 'Habooba, that's not fair. Why is the kitchen only for girls? What if I like doing the stuff outside as well? Don't you think that is a bit unfair?'

Habooba locked eyes with her granddaughter. 'How do you think you're going to get married if you don't know how to cook, *ya habiba*?'

Kissing her teeth, Layla glowered. 'Habooba what are you talking about? I'm too young to even be thinking about marriage. And anyway, what about my personality?'

Habooba smiled. 'Don't be silly, ya Layla. It's never too early to start getting marriage ready. *Yallah*, get started on the vegetables, *mumkin*?'

Layla's mouth twisted in frustration. 'I really don't like it, ya Habooba, I really don't!'

Habooba turned to look at her granddaughter, eyebrow lifted, not moving away from the stove, then swivelled back to face the pot she was stirring.

'What don't you like, ya Layla?' Habooba prompted.

Layla huffed. 'I just don't know why there's so much that's girls' stuff and boys' stuff here. All the fun stuff is the boys' stuff too – adventures, being the boss, anything that's *cool* gets to be done by boys. It's not fair! No one ever asks Ozzie what he's doing about getting married, either. And he never gets in trouble for breaking the rules! I don't want to be stuck in the kitchen, serving everyone else, living the way other people decide and not getting to live my own life.'

'Lay–' Habooba started to reply, but Layla cut her off.

'I mean, at least in Australia I can wiggle my way out of things, but I don't understand it here, I just don't. Why can't I do things on my own? Why can't I decide what I want to do by myself? I just . . . I just . . .'

Layla ran out of air, hunching over the stool, defeated. All the events of the last few days had caught up with her – the abrupt flight to Sudan, visiting her grandmother in hospital, learning about the protest, being grounded, not being a part of the GDT any more. It was *a lot*.

Habooba turned the gas down on the stove and came to perch on another stool next to Layla. Gently, with her hand in a fist, she rubbed Layla's back soothingly. '*Habiba, habiba, habiba* . . .'

'I just don't get it, ya Habooba. I don't understand why things are the way they are here, but then I feel so guilty, because if I don't like the way things are, does that mean I am less Sudaniya? Yousra always says to me that I'm not Sudaniya enough, but I don't even really know what it means to be Sudaniya any more. Isn't the fact that I was born here enough? I know my tongue is heavy and I can't really cook, and I want to do all the things the boys do and my *sum3a*, my reputation, is probably terrible. I'm scared if I don't like all the things that a Sudaniya is supposed to do, then maybe it means I am not really Sudaniya?'

With that, Habooba rocked back on her haunches and let out a loud laugh. Layla looked at her grandmother, shocked.

'Habooba!' Layla shot out indignantly. 'What are you laughing about? This is no laughing matter!'

Her grandmother continued to laugh for a bit, before eventually catching her breath and replying. 'Layla, *habiba*, of course you're Sudaniya. You were born in Sudan, your father is Dongolawi and your mother is Halfawiya. *Habiba*, your blood is strong with the blood of the Nubian Queens – the Kandakaat from the Kingdom of Kush. All of that is what makes you Sudanese, not whether you cook or the length of your hair or what you like to do in your spare time.'

Layla was still frowning, but at this she sniffed, wiping the snot from her nose. A single slime strand had fallen onto the table so Layla hurriedly wiped that up too.

Why does my crying never seem as graceful as those people on TV?

Looking back at her grandmother, who wore an expression of bemusement, she began again. 'What do you mean, Habooba? Two minutes ago you were just saying boys do this and girls do that, and I swear you said that I will never get married without learning how to cook. Also, what's cooking got to do with marriage anyway?'

Ooof, I'm getting a bit confused by everything that's going on.

'I might have the blood of a Sudaniya, but I live in Australia now. Does that mean because I don't have the blood of an Australian, I'm not Australian either? Plus, who are these Kandakaat you're talking about anyway?' Layla let out a ragged sigh as her grandmother got back up to tend to the cooking. 'Why is this stuff so *hard*, ya Habooba?'

Habooba smiled to herself. 'Ah, the Kandakaat! Hasn't your mother told you about these women? What do you know about the Ancient Kingdom of Kush, *ya banoota*?'

Layla shook her head. She'd never heard of this Kush place before.

'The Ancient Kingdom of Kush is where we are descended from. You know how Egypt has pyramids and there were Pharaohs long ago?'

Layla nodded.

'Well, we had our own version. We actually have more pyramids than the Egyptians have!'

At this Layla's expression brightened a tiny bit. That was pretty cool.

'The kingdom lasted for over fourteen hundred years and was wealthy and prosperous. And the kingdom was often run by women. A Kandaka was a strong and powerful leader whom the people respected. Kandakaat had beautiful names, like Shanakdakhete, Amanirenas, Amanishakheto and Khennuwa. They charted their own paths and decided who they wanted to be and how they wanted to run the kingdom. Didn't you say you had some saying that got you through the hard times?'

'Channel the *jamel* . . .' Layla offered.

'Yes, well, really it should be channel the Kandaka!'

Layla appreciated her grandmother's attempt to come up with a new mantra, even though it didn't rhyme.

Habooba continued. 'Sadly, the kingdom and the language died out around 400 BC, which was a century or so before the Prophet Mohammed (SAW) was born.'

'Oh, what's left?' Layla asked.

'The bare bones now really. The Europeans came and stole most of the gold and treasures that were inside the pyramids, but that's a story for a different time.'

Layla's eyes widened at all this new information. 'So, we come from strong and powerful queens?'

'Yes, *habiba*. And there is a strong place for the woman and the queen in our society. What women do *is* important.' Habooba smirked. 'So, if women are in the kitchen, then the kitchen is important.'

Layla wasn't believing that so easily. 'Hmm, I don't know, Habooba. That's not how it's seen in Australia; I don't think I've heard anyone say that. "Get into the kitchen" is used to insult women.'

'I don't know what it's like for you, *ya habiba*. It must be complicated living in Australia. Maybe they have different ideas of what is important. But our family is Sudanese, and the spirit of the

Kandaka is in our blood. It's in your blood too, even if your tongue is heavy and your *bamiya* is burnt. But at the end of the day, it's up to you. You can choose to be more Sudanese, more Australian, or both, even none at all.'

'None at all?!'

'*Yallah*. The thing to remember, *ya habiba*, is that things have also changed a lot in the last few years. We're not quite living in the Kingdom of Kush any more, even though their spirit runs in our blood. Here in modern Sudan there are expectations of how things are done, and they help people make sense of the world, because there are lots of other things that don't work. Does that make sense?'

Layla shook her head.

'Well, think about it this way,' Habooba's voice heaved with effort as she used the *mufraka* on the *mulaa7*, rolling the handle of the wooden kitchen utensil between the palms of her hands, the tight twists breaking up the chunks in the stew.

Should Habooba be putting in that much effort when she just got out of the hospital? Layla thought about saying something, then decided against it. Habooba took directions from no one.

'Who makes the rules in Australia that everyone needs to follow?' her grandmother asked.

'Mmm, the government?'

'And how did the government get in?'

'Well, people voted for them.'

'And what happens if they don't do their job?'

'We vote them out!'

'Exactly. But we can't do that in this country, not at the moment, anyway. And it's a problem, because the government here, well, it hasn't really been taking care of the people for many, many years. And so, if the government isn't going to take care of the people, people need to take care of each other, right? When you take care of each other, you have to make rules for everyone to follow, right? Like in your family, you have rules for who does the dishes, who does the mowing, *mushkida*?'

Layla nodded slowly, kinda making sense of it.

'People start to find ways to organise themselves without the government. How? By making and following rules that they think are good for society and for keeping things going. But it's not really about what's wrong and what's right, because not all these rules are wrong or right.

It's more about how people make sense of the world around them.'

'So, Habooba, are you saying that people think girls should be in the kitchen not because it's the right thing, but because that's a way for them to keep society going?'

Habooba turned to Layla, still beating the *mulaa7* with the *mufraka*. 'Mmm, something like that.' Habooba whipped her braid around so it wouldn't dangle in the pot. 'People find ways to make sense of the world, and then that becomes normal. But, just because it's "normal", it doesn't mean it's right. And just because it's what everyone else does, it doesn't mean you have to do it too.'

'Well, Habooba, if you think this, why are you making me work in the kitchen?'

Habooba laughed, a guffaw that echoed around the kitchen. 'Because you were running around with nothing better to do!'

Layla grinned. On that point, her grandmother was right.

'Ya Layla, things are changing, of course. I followed the way things were laid out for me, and then did other things on top of that. That was the way it worked for my generation: if I got married and did well in the kitchen, then people would say I had a good reputation, and then after that I could do what I liked. And that's what I did. I went back to school, but only after I had your mother and the rest of the kids. I found a way to make the system work for me. We did this so that your generation would have it easier. Look at your mother. She moved to a different country and built a life there! That would have been very difficult for me to do. But *Alhamdulilah*, every generation has its own battles. It sounds like your battle is figuring out where you want to belong.'

Where I want to belong? But it's not where I want to belong, it's who will accept me, right? Isn't that how belonging works?

'But, Habooba, how am I supposed to decide that? Isn't it for other people to tell me?'

'*Habiba*, it's up to you to decide who you want to be. No one can take that choice away from you.'

Habooba turned back around to the pot, indicating the conversation was over. 'Now, are you going to get started on those vegetables or what? And not because you're a girl, but because I want you to.'

Layla chuckled, sniffled and then picked up the knife.

What does she mean, I choose where I belong? How am I supposed to know whether or not I belong somewhere?

Layla knew that the blood in her veins meant something . . .

What about Australia? Another voice in Layla's head asked.

Aw shhhh, she told herself. She'd figure that out later.

CHAPTER 17

THE next day Layla and her siblings, cousins, aunts and uncles, along with Habooba all sat around the table, quietly eating lunch. Everyone was silent, concentrating on their food, lost in their own thoughts. The air was unseasonably still: it felt like the calm before the storm.

Today was the day of the *millyoneeya*.

'What's the *millyoneeya*?' Sami asked Layla, his small voice cutting through the thoughtful air.

'Ah, I think it's a big version of the protests. Maybe someone else can explain?' Layla asked, looking around at the table.

Ma'ab and Mohammed had food in their mouths, Yousra was secretly on her phone and Kareem had his head in a newspaper.

'The *millyoneeya* is the biggest protest march planned yet,' offered Marwan, when he saw no one else was jumping in to respond.

'Everyone in the whole of Sudan is coming out,' Ozzie added.

Ma'ab and Mohammed nodded vigorously, and Ma'ab finished swallowing a mouthful of *fool* before adding to the conversation. 'There are buses from Darfur, El-Obeid, Kassala and even a train from Atbara.'

Kareem lowered the newspaper from his face. 'The train from Atbara is coming?' he asked, incredulous. 'Wow, my father worked on that refurbishment.' His voice was wistful for a moment. 'I remember running around his workshop as a baby. Amazing that the *nas* Atbara are coming all the way down.'

'Some people have even walked hundreds of miles to be at the *millyoneeya*,' Mohammed added.

This sounds so incredible. Layla turned to look at her father out of the corner of her eye.

'Don't even think about it!' he warned, before she could open her mouth.

'But, Baba, everyone is going! Even you and Mama and Yousra, and you're going to take Sami and Yousif too! You said yourself it's a historic moment, why won't you let me be a part of it?'

Kareem shook his head. He was a resolute man when he was cross. 'You should have thought about that before you focused on yourself and chose to ignore what I told you to do.'

Layla pouted, folding her arms and slumping in her seat, the fried Nile perch on her plate forgotten.

'I would have been able to stay on the team and be there for Habooba just fine,' she muttered under her breath.

'You just don't learn, do you, Layla?' Kareem responded, shaking his head.

'Don't worry, Layla. We will take lots of photos for you,' Sami said, trying to cheer his sister up.

But Layla knew it wasn't enough. She felt powerless.

Ya Allah!

The *dhuhur athan* rang its way through the

city, the sonorous calls echoing and overlapping one another, harmonies ricocheting through the streets of Khartoum. As the first notes of the call to prayer hit the air, the boys and men at the table polished off the last bits of food in their hands and stood up, getting ready to head to the mosque. It was *jum3ah*, the weekly collective prayer compulsory for all men to attend. The *Imam* would deliver a *khutbah*, a sermon, one that was hopefully relevant to the community. The *khutbahs* were how information was distributed among the communities and villages. It was a very effective way of getting the word out. And today, the word was strong.

'We will meet all the women at the *qiyadah* later,' Ozzie called out to the family left at the dining table, referencing the sit-in that had become the heartbeat of the protests.

'Stay safe, *ya shabab*, stay safe!' Khaltu Amal called from the table, her face creased with worry.

Layla looked at who was left: Khaltu Amal, Mama, Habooba, Yousra and the twins.

Maybe I can try one more time?

'Can I come with you and Yousra?' she asked Khaltu Amal.

Fadia interrupted before Amal could reply. 'It's not your fight, ya Layla. The airport is meant to be opening up briefly in the next few days, so we will be leaving soon anyway,' Fadia said.

'It *is* my fight,' Layla said.

'It's not,' Fadia responded, clearly exasperated by the conversation.

'It is, I'm Sudaniya!'

'*Bilahi?*' Fadia's tone switched to something more acerbic. 'You knew nothing about Sudan's politics before we came here. You didn't even want to come and see your sick grandmother! All you cared about was your competition, and after a week here, now you think you're a Kandaka?'

Layla was shocked into silence.

'Layla, *habiba*, we left everything here in Sudan to build a better life for you in Australia. We didn't risk it all so that you would come back and put your life on the line for the same battles we fought decades ago,' her mother said.

'But that is not your choice to make on their behalf.' Habooba joined the conversation, her voice soft but powerful. She was the ultimate authority in the household.

But Fadia wasn't finished. 'Yes, ya Mama, but

she is still a child. My child. And both Kareem and I are agreed on this. *Khalas*.'

Meeting Layla's eyes, Fadia made those rules very clear.

'You are not going out to the *millyoneeya* today, Layla. You are to stay inside and keep yourself busy. Maybe start packing. We're going to leave on the first flight out of the city.'

Layla stood up abruptly and fled the table.

I can't believe this, I can't believe this, I can't believe this.

Layla flung herself onto the thin mattress, slamming the door shut behind her, her face flushed with tears of anger.

What does she mean, this isn't my fight? Why doesn't she want to let me go? Doesn't she know I can take care of myself?

Layla was not happy. Not happy at all.

After a few moments alone, Yousra slipped into the bedroom, gently closing the door behind her. She sat on the edge of the bed, rubbing Layla's back.

'*Shhh, habiba*, it's okay. I'll stay with you and maybe it's for the best, you know? Keep us safe. I can maybe even ask Fareed to come visit, you can finally meet him.'

'Keep us all safe?' Layla twisted around to face her cousin, her fury causing her to ignore the comment about Fareed. 'No, they just want to hide us girls away. The boys get to go out and fight.'

'Yeh, but they are boys, ya Layla.'

'I don't care! It shouldn't matter anyway. Plus, I'm old enough to decide what I want to fight for.'

Yousra pursed her lips. 'Layla, you've only been here a hot minute. This is fun and exciting for you, but these are our *lives*. This is not a game.'

Layla couldn't believe what she was hearing. She rolled around on the bed again, spurning her cousin.

Wow. No one takes me seriously.

Channel the Kandaka, Habooba had told her. What would a Kandaka do?

Well, they certainly wouldn't give up at the first hurdle.

After a few minutes of furious silence, Layla

came up with a plan. She turned back to Yousra, who was on the phone with Fareed (*obvs, she was always on the phone to Fareed*).

'Yousra,' Layla whispered.

Her cousin shot her an annoyed glance, silently telling her to be quiet.

'Yousra!' Layla whispered again, louder.

'Just one second, Ahmed, my cousin is trying to talk to me,' Yousra whispered on the phone to the boy in a silky, smooth voice. Her tone instantly shifted as she switched focus and spoke to Layla. 'What?!' she demanded, her voice neither smooth nor silky.

'I've got an . . . wait. Who is Ahmed?'

'None of your business! Now, what's up?'

'I've got an idea,' Layla said.

Yousra raised a single eyebrow.

Layla continued. 'Tell me how you sneak out when you meet Fareed . . . or Ahmed or whoever.'

Yousra's eyebrows knotted together. 'I can show you, but why?'

Layla's face split into a toothy grin. 'Why don't we sneak out to the *millyoneeya*?'

Such a good idea!

'That's a terrible idea!' Yousra whispered right back. 'And keep your voice down. We would get into *so much* trouble if they found out, you know?'

'Yeh, like the same amount of trouble you'll get into if I tell Khalu Marwan about your *jiks*? Or the many *jakasi* in your life – how many do you have now? Where do you even find these guys?'

Yousra smiled slyly. 'You've gotta play the field, *habibi*, keep them on their toes.'

Layla chuckled and shook her head. 'Anyway, that's not important. Don't you want to be there?' Layla tried a different tack. 'Is this Ahmed guy going to be at the *qiyadah*?'

Yousra studied her cousin warily. 'Maybe . . .'

'Well, why don't we just meet up with him? I wanna meet these boyfriends of yours. Maybe we can take some photos or something and then come back home. No one will even notice! It's being a part of history, ya Yousra. Isn't that something to be proud of?'

'*Rasik nashif, mushkida?*' Yousra exclaimed.

She's coming around . . .

'But we're all a bit stubborn like that, aren't we?' Layla replied. 'And it's for a good cause, it's for Sudan!'

Yousra shrugged. 'Yeh, it's for Sudan. But why are you so obsessed with going to these protests anyway? Is it really worth sneaking out and getting in trouble again?'

'Let's not think about that right now, Yousra. Let's just go. Be a part of history. I'm sick of being grounded, sick of being told what I can and can't do. Sick of doing nothing but kitchen work. C'mon, cousin. Be with me on this. Channel your inner Kandaka!'

Yousra relented. 'Okay. Fine. Just don't get *me* into trouble again. Let me call Ahmed back.'

CHAPTER 18

LAYLA and her cousin had to wait until their mothers left the house before putting their plan into action. To keep the pretence up, Layla stayed curled up in bed, pretending she was asleep. Yousra sat in front of the TV, secretly on her phone.

Eventually, Khaltu Amal walked in to check on Layla.

'Layla, *habiba*,' Khaltu Amal cooed, perching lightly on the edge of the *3angareb*. 'Are you okay?'

Layla stayed quiet, back still to her aunt, facing the wall in a fetal position.

Amal continued in her soothing voice. 'It's okay, Layla. Your mum says some strong words, but you know she cares about you.'

Layla scoffed only half-jokingly, rolling her eyes under her lids.

Amal noticed and smiled slightly. 'She just wanted to protect you, okay?' Amal stood up, straightening her *toub*. 'Now, we're heading out. Habooba is going to stay back, it's too much for her to travel so soon after the hospital. Your mum is going to come with me so I'm not on my own, even though we both know she doesn't really want to.' This last part was whispered, like a secret between the two. 'Yousra has said she's happy to stay home, so you're not alone. You can watch the *millyoneeya* on TV,' Amal hummed affectionately, rubbing Layla's back softly one last time. 'The view will probably be better from the TV anyway, *habiba*.'

Amal kissed Layla lightly on her forehead, and left the room.

Layla waited, straining to listen to Amal and Fadia discuss about how cold it was going to get outside, where they should meet the men, whether they should take snacks. After the conversation lasted for what felt like a lifetime, Layla heard the ladies call out goodbye to Yousra, shut the front door, pile into the car and drive off.

Layla realised her mum didn't even say bye to her. To be fair, she wasn't sure what she would have said to Mama at that point. But still, the snub hurt.

As soon as they were out, Yousra bounded back into the room and onto the bed with Layla.

'Okay, so Habooba should be asleep in the next hour. You stay here, I'll keep her busy, then come back in when we're ready to go,' Yousra whispered excitedly.

'I'm glad you're enthusiastic now,' Layla said, only half-jokingly.

'Both Ahmed *and* Fareed said they would meet us at the *qiyadah*, so you finally get to meet them.'

The *qiyadah*! Layla couldn't wait to visit the famous square. She'd heard and seen so much about it; there had been a school set up, little shops, tea vendors and even a hospital, all in front of the military headquarters. In all the pictures, it looked colourful and peaceful and fun and exactly like the way Sudanese people wanted Sudan to be. Layla couldn't wait to check it out.

Her cousin continued, excitement bubbling over. 'It *is* the *millyoneeya*. See you in a bit.'

Yousra was on a mission!

Layla was finally pleased. She was doing something she wanted to do, something that felt *important,* and it didn't matter if she got in trouble for it. She was in a ton of trouble anyway. How much worse could it get?

Once the coast was clear, Yousra ran back into the room. 'Okay, we gotta be quiet, but *yallah*!'

Layla flipped around, excited. She bit her lip and grinned.

'What should I wear?!' Layla wondered.

Before she said another word, Yousra put a finger to her lips. She was all over it. The fifteen-year-old had already prepped her younger cousin the perfect protest outfit: big gold disk earrings and a long-sleeved T-shirt with a raised revolutionary fist on the front in the colours of the old Sudanese flag – blue, yellow and green. Layla beamed and then paired the top with a billowing black skirt and a bumbag containing supplies, just in case.

'Where did you get all that *stuff?*' Yousra asked incredulously, as Layla rammed snacks, money and a first-aid kit into her bumbag.

Layla chuckled. 'I'm an inventor, *habiba*. I like to be prepared.'

Yousra laughed. 'You're a funny one, *ya Australeeya*.'

As they dressed, Yousra narrated the path they would take. 'We will go out the back door of the house, past the dusty shed, over the back fence (the only section without barbed wire on top) and that will take us to the *zugaga* behind the mosque.'

Layla nodded, committing her cousin's instructions to memory.

By the time they snuck out of the house, being careful not to wake Habooba up, the night had deepened, with only a sprinkling of bright stars making an appearance. The girls used the lights on their phones to illuminate the way.

Everything was dark and still, like the city itself was holding its breath. There were no street lights in the alley, only the faint green glow from the mosque's neon sign illuminating their path. Walking through the small dusty *zugaga* behind

Yousra, Layla tried to act cool, like she hadn't just snuck out of her house to join a once-in-a-lifetime protest against the express orders of her parents. She reminded herself to be casual, but there was nothing casual about this situation in the slightest.

Reaching the main street, Layla, in an effort to continue acting cool, attempted to hail a *raksha*.

Immediately, Yousra stopped her. 'Ya Layla, why? Any of the buses will take us to the protest, they're all going that way.'

'Oh!' It was true. Looking around, Layla realised that every single bus on the road was packed to the brim with people flying flags, throwing up the peace sign, ('Here it means *madaneeya*, okay?' Yousra clarified.) carrying posters and chanting the same freedom chants that Layla had been listening to in the WhatsApp protest videos. The air thrummed with anticipation. People were everywhere, waving out of bus windows and beeping their car horns, emitting an infectious energy that Layla had never felt before. She imagined it was somewhat like going to an important football match, like the final of the FIFA World Cup on your home soil. But it also felt more important than that; it felt urgent, vital, like people's lives depended on it. Not for the first time, Layla was struck by how different this felt to the marches she had seen in Australia, but she couldn't quite figure out why. Was it just that everyone looked Sudanese?

'*Yallah*, Layla!' Yousra had hailed a bus, and they squeezed themselves on, standing in the central aisle and joining the chanting. '*7ureya, salam wa 3adala! Madaneeya khiyar alsha3b!*'

Over and over and over again they chanted, until it felt like they were part of the chant and the chant was part of them.

'When do we get off?' asked Layla.

'When everyone else does,' Yousra said, smiling.

Soon, the bus stopped and riders spilled out onto the footpath, greeted by the most fantastic sight. The dark cloak of night had been punctured by stadium-like lights set up by protestors, the earlier stillness and silence of the neighbourhood nowhere to be seen. It was all movement and noise, creative chaos, intimate and intimidating all at the same time. Every single soul in Khartoum was out on the streets, either in body or spirit.

They had arrived.

Layla couldn't believe her eyes. All her worries –
being grounded, Habooba's health, the GDT – fled
her mind, and she was fully and wholly present.
Bodies pressed up against them as the two girls
made their way through the crowd, not so much
walking, but more being carried along by a human
wave. There could have been a million people
there, maybe even more! People hanging off light-
poles, sitting on top of billboards and watching
the huge screen set up just outside the *qiyadah*
that was streaming news and videos from the
sit-in area. It was the Ekka, the Olympics and
the coronation of a Kandaka, all at the same time.

'Are we going to be able to get to the main
sit-in?' asked Layla. They had been dropped off a
short distance away from the sit-in, but entering
the heart of the *qiyadah* was proving to be a
challenge. Yousra didn't reply.

Layla realised she had quite a lot of questions.
'Are we going to be able to find anyone? How
will we meet up with Ahmed and Fareed?' *Wait.*
'Are we going to meet them both at the same
time? Have they ever met each other?' Layla
chuckled at the absurdity of dealing with Yousra's
love life amidst a revolution.

'Let me send a drop pin to the boys. I might message Ozzie and Mohammed and Ma'ab as well.' Yousra replied, ignoring her cousin's interrogation. 'I won't message Mama, don't worry.'

Layla poked her tongue out in reply. She noticed the noise levels were starting to pick up, but it all seemed pretty celebratory.

There was nothing for Mama to be worried about, it will all be fine. I can't believe I'm out here, part of making a change!

Peering up ahead, Layla noticed two women in white *toubs* standing on top of a car and serenading the audience. The women were young, only a few years older than Layla, but they really did seem like Kandakaat, standing high above the crowd, leading the call and response chanting of the protesters.

Layla felt drawn to the women, her feet involuntarily taking her towards the lively, passionate throng. While it was quite dark, past *3isha* now, there were enough lights on that Layla could make out where she needed to go.

'Layla, stop!' Yousra's voice was barely audible.

'*MADANEYAAAA!*' The call for civilian rule surrounded them.

'Layla!' Yousra yelled again.

Layla turned around to see her cousin had fallen way behind, a horde of people suddenly coming between the two of them.

Yousra sounded stressed as she yelled across the din. 'Come back! You can't just go off and leave me, Layla. We're by ourselves and my phone's stopped working. There are too many people here! We have to stick together.'

Layla nodded, though she wasn't sure why Yousra was so upset. Her mood had completely flipped. It was all a big adventure, wasn't it? 'Oh, it's okay, *habiba*,' she yelled, craning her neck as Yousra bobbed in and out of view. 'I'm coming right back.'

A group of people abruptly swelled around them and Layla lost sight of her cousin.

'Yousra?' she called, trying to make her voice heard over the commotion. 'Yousra? YOUSRA?!'

There was no response.

CHAPTER 19

LAYLA spun around, completely discombobu-
lated. *Where did she go?!*

'Yousra? Yousra!' she called, but her voice was
swept up and scattered, sand grains in a desert.

Then, suddenly, someone tapped her on the
shoulder, whispering in her ear. 'Layla?'

Wait, who is that?

'Hello?' Layla pivoted on the spot. 'Who is
it?' All she could see for a moment was a silhou-
ette. As her eyes adjusted, she recognised the face.
'Ma'ab!'

Alhamdulilah, *my cousin.* Her face collapsed

into relief. For a second, she thought she had been caught by her dad, *again*!

Ma'ab, in a dark blue T-shirt and a Sudani flag, also wore a mildly confused expression. 'What are you doing here? Didn't Khalu say you were grounded? How did you even get out?'

'Oh, yeh. About that . . .' Layla avoided eye contact with her tall cousin. 'I just had to come and see the *qiyadah* for myself! Caught a *7afla* and everything.'

Ma'ab laughed and squeezed Layla's shoulder. 'You're trouble, you are. Are you by yourself?'

'No, she's with me,' interrupted Yousra, who had pushed through from behind a clump of protesters. Yousra grabbed her cousin's hand. 'Don't do that again, okay?' Yousra's tone was stern. This was a demand, not a suggestion.

Layla nodded, her expression apologetic.

'Yousra, you're here too! Ah, makes sense. Well, we might as well find the others. Better to be together.'

Layla felt unsure – she had wanted to come out to the protests anonymously, sneak back home before they got caught, but it seemed the jig was up. Looking at Yousra, Layla realised that she didn't really have an option.

'Really?' Layla whispered.

'Layla, I can't deal with you just disappearing. If we stick with them, we're much better protected.'

Layla swallowed and fiddled with her bumbag, complying with a small nod.

'*Yallah*. Let's go!' shouted Ma'ab, and they all pressed forward.

Masses of people moved around them, like they were all ants in a colony, walking towards the nest. Layla felt surprisingly safe in the wave of people enveloping her, like falling into a warm and intimate hug. This was no cuddle from a mother or best friend though, this was the embrace of her fellow country people all united in the fight for freedom. She saw kids running around, playing games with each other, she saw grandparents being wheeled about in wheelchairs, folks with walking sticks, on people's shoulders. Young, old, rich, poor, dark skin, light skin, *toub* or western dressing, everyone was there, and everyone was in the fight for a better, more united Sudan. Layla suddenly felt an urge to yell out, share her truth with the world and her kinfolk as witness.

'*Ana Sudaniya!* I am Sudanese,' Layla burst out, beaming.

Yousra squeezed right beside. Layla turned to her cousin, bemused. 'Yeh?'

'YEH!'

'*Inti Sudaniya.*' Yousra affirmed her cousin's declaration and smiled.

The two paused in the crowd to give each other a hug, holding tight for a moment. When they let go, Ma'ab had disappeared.

'Ma'ab? Ma'ab! Where did he go?' Yousra yelped. Two family members vanishing before her eyes within minutes was fraying her vocal cords – and patience.

They'd had him in sight, but now he had melted completely into the crowd. Layla and Yousra searched the faces around them.

'Is that him?' Layla pointed to a lanky figure in the Sudani flag standing on a concrete block a couple of meters ahead.

Yes! It was Ma'ab. He was combing the crowd for any sign of Layla and Yousra, and making eye contact, he waved.

'Come over,' he called. 'I'm just getting some water. Do you want a drink?'

Yousra and Layla both nodded vigorously, their panic dissolving.

'Yeh, I'm parched as!' Layla yelled.

'Yes, please. *Shukran*,' Yousra called, trying to make herself heard. They pressed towards him, the adventure continuing.

Suddenly the electricity went out.

The entire area was plunged into deep darkness, and there was silence for an instant; a brief moment, a collective holding of breath.

Layla's heart skipped a beat. She squeezed her eyes shut, hoping it was just a dream, but no. When she opened them again, she could barely see her own fingers in front of her face. *What is happening? What is happening?*

Layla couldn't think.

Ya Allah, please let this be a nightmare, please wake me up.

Time stood still.

And then, just as suddenly as it was cast, the spell broke.

BANG! BANG! BANG!

Shouts and high-pitched screams filled the air. Everyone panicked, all at the same time, transforming the *qiyadah* into a mosh pit of terror. The citizens who had come to this peaceful protest in good faith, to demand that their government step down to make way for a brighter future, were all now terrified for their lives.

BANG!

Folks were running every which way, charging into each other, fleeing without direction, blinded by the loss of light, fear and the memories of the tyranny this government was known for. Horror was etched on every face, expressions of people in a desperate search for safety. But where was safe?

Layla's mind went blank, completely unable to deal with the scenes around her. It was like she was in Shutdown Mode, but someone else had switched her off.

Okay, there's no light. No light. No light. We need light. Layla tried to open her bumbag, but her hands wouldn't move! She stared down at them, willing her hands to shift, but nothing was happening. She tried to move her feet, but they too were rooted to the ground, stuck like she had stepped in wet cement. Time stretched like molasses. Had it been seconds, or hours, that she'd been frozen?

Layla bit her lip, then realised what else was missing.

Where was Yousra? Where was Ma'ab? Layla opened her mouth to scream, but nothing came out.

Ya Allah, *help me!*

Suddenly a tall, broad boy ran headlong into Layla before pushing her aside and continuing to sprint. 'They're coming!' he yelled in Layla's direction in Arabic. 'Go! *Yallah!* Run!'

WHO is coming?

Layla, head spinning from the collision, scoured the landscape around her trying to gain her bearings. 'Yousra? Yousra!' she called, her vocal cords finally working.

A hand squeezed Layla's, and she turned to see Yousra's eyes reflecting her own fear. Layla squeezed her hand right back. Then a clatter and a loud hiss behind them, as smoke – or tear gas? – started to fill the space all around. Layla's eyes stinging.

'Don't rub your eyes!' Yousra yelled.

Layla nodded, eyes and nose streaming, she tried to blink, to see what was going on around her. People were still running, some dispersing and scuttling into side streets, some crouched in corners, struck down by tear gas, everyone trying to get away from the centre of the *qiyadah*. The electricity was still out so the darkness hadn't lifted, but the occasional flash of light from protestors' torches pierced the blanket of night. The blood-curdling yells from the direction of the military HQ were getting louder though, and closer.

Layla searched around for somewhere to hide, somewhere to stay safe – she couldn't see a thing, and her eyes were stinging! – but before she could move, Yousra had sunk to her knees, eyes tightly shut and hands over her ears, trembling.

Oh no, she's not okay . . .

Kneeling down, Layla wrapped herself around her cousin, hiding Yousra, protecting her from the surrounding anarchy. Layla's heart was racing at a million miles a minute. She could feel the blood coursing through her body, laced with adrenalin and revolution. As she sat with her cousin, Layla prayed for it all be over. *Ya Allah.*

Then as abruptly as it had been cut off, the electricity flickered back on. Layla breathed an audible sigh of relief. The tension seemed to lift slightly as people began to slow down and look around, trying to gauge the level of danger. If there was light, surely that meant things were all right?

But any relief was short lived, as Layla noticed the body of a boy lying on the ground a few meters in front of her. He was in a blue T-shirt with the Sudani flag wrapped around him. The boy was covered in blood.

Still holding onto Yousra in the fetal position on the ground, Layla shut her eyes tightly, praying that she would wake up from this bad dream, this nightmare.

Layla opened her eyes, but this time, her prayer had not been answered.

Because she recognised the motionless body lying just out of reach.

It was Ma'ab.

No.

No.

No.

NO!!!

CHAPTER 20

'YOUSRA! YOUSRA! YOUSRA!' Layla bellowed, trying to wake her cousin out of her stupor. When Yousra didn't respond, Layla left her and ran over to Ma'ab.

What do I do? What do I do?

Layla's hands were shaking, tears streaming down her face, dripping onto Ma'ab's shirt. *C'mon!* She willed the seized cogs in her brain to start turning again. Layla put her ear on Ma'ab's chest, trying to see if she could hear a heartbeat. Was he still alive?

'*Dug-dug, dug-dug,*' she heard, and almost breathed a sigh of relief before she realised that noise was *her own* heart thumping so loudly she couldn't hear anything else.

'HELP!' she yelled out in English. 'We need *help*!' she yelled out again, in Arabic, and a few people running by looked over, quickly joining Layla.

'I think he's hurt,' Layla whispered to the two men.

They nodded and then lifted up Ma'ab's limp body, each of his arms over one of their shoulders, blood soaking the Sudanese flag. 'We'll take him to the hospital,' they assured Layla.

'Should I come with you?' Layla called after them, but they'd already scurried off, hurrying towards the ambulances that had arrived at the scene. Layla fell to her knees, her mind blank.

Then, out of nowhere, puffing with exertion, Mohammed appeared, his face petrified, the whites of his eyes showing.

'*Layla!*' he yelled. '*Shufti Ma'ab?* I heard shots and I thought he was near here.' Mohammed wasn't focused on Layla, his attention jagged and splintered, a twin in a desperate search for their other half.

Layla's heart squeezed, and she pointed into the distance. 'See that flag? That's him. They're taking him to the hospital.'

Before she'd even finished the sentence, Mohammed was off and running. 'MA'AB! I'm coming to the hospital, that's my twin! That's my brother!'

Relieved that someone from the family was going with Ma'ab to the hospital, Layla took in a ragged breath. She turned around on the spot, disoriented, searching for Yousra. Her cousin was still in a ball on the ground. As Layla walked towards Yousra, it all began to hit her. The memory of Ma'ab covered in blood, the heaviness of his motionless body, the smell of the gunpowder – it was all overwhelming. Layla clenched her jaw and her eyes began overflowing with tears.

I'm so sorry, Ma'ab.

She moved slowly back to her cousin, kneeling down beside her. As Layla hugged Yousra once more, Yousra shuddered. 'Your hands are wet, Layla,' she whispered.

Layla looked down. It was Ma'ab's blood.

Layla gulped, her dry throat convulsing. She balled up her fists, shifting around to be back to back with Yousra, their spines touching as they both curled up into themselves. Layla lowered her head into her chest, wrapped her arms around her folded legs and burst into racking, heaving tears.

Layla and Yousra were found soon after by Kareem, Khalu Marwan and Ozzie. Mohammed had phoned his dad to update them on the news about Ma'ab. By the time the rescue party arrived, Layla had stopped crying and Yousra had slowly come back to the present. Layla had convinced her to move to a place out of the line of fire.

'Not too far, I can't go too far,' Yousra had said, and Layla agreed. They settled in the first alley they could find, sitting underneath a tree, facing each other and waiting silently, while holding hands. Yousra's phone had run out of battery, but her location pin had gone through just before it went flat, so they knew they would be found here.

When the men arrived, Layla flinched, waiting for the rebuke from her father. It didn't come. He completely ignored her. In fact, he was silent the whole time. It was Khalu Marwan who spoke.

'How are you?' he asked, and then peered closer at Layla. 'Layla, you're covered in blood. Should we take you to hospital?'

For Layla, it was all too much. She burst into tears again, hiding her face in her elbow, sniffling loudly.

Things happened swiftly after that. Khalu Marwan sent Ozzie home with the girls and set off to the hospital with Kareem. Layla's father was immediately on the phone to his wife.

'Yes, we found them. They're safe, *Alhamdulilah*. Do you know what hospital they sent all the injured to? Head there now. Yes, Ma'ab has been shot. I don't know. I don't know. We're on our way there now. *Khair Inshallah.*'

As they organised how to get to their various destinations, Layla stopped sniffling. 'Can we come?' she asked, wanting to be at the hospital. She wasn't sure why, but it felt like the right thing to do.

'Are you out of your mind?' Kareem turned around to Layla, snapping. 'Have you *completely* lost it?' His voice rose, harder and sharper than Layla had ever heard it before. 'This is *not* a game, ya Layla! You shouldn't be out here. You could have been *killed*. Go with your brother back home, and we will deal with you later.'

Layla swayed a little, stunned by the force of her father's rebuke.

'C'mon,' Ozzie said quietly to his sister. '*Yallah*, both of you. Let's go home.' With that, he grabbed their arms just above the elbow and steered them out of the little *zugaga*, towards the main road. Before Layla could even open her mouth, Ozzie said, 'We're getting a taxi. Now *shhh*.'

They were silent on the drive home. In the front seat, Ozzie whispered instructions to the driver. In the back seat, Yousra and Layla looked out their respective windows, but their arms were outstretched towards each other, hands clasped together.

Layla didn't say a word.

When the taxi turned into their street, their neighbourhood was dark, eerie. The stillness was worlds away from the chaos of the *qiyadah*. Layla felt like she was in a dream.

Ozzie tipped the driver handsomely, thanking him for getting them to their house safely. 'Stay safe, *3mu*,' he said through the window, tapping the car door. The driver, an old man wearing a *3imma*, nodded respectfully and drove off.

Ozzie fumbled with the keys for the blue metal gate, the noise echoing up and down the street. Yousra had let go of Layla's hand and now wrapped her hands around her torso, like she was holding herself in. As soon as they were through the door, she bolted up the patio stairs and into the house. The sounds of retching bounced off the walls.

Layla noticed that all the lights were off, save for the bedroom bulb that Yousra had just switched on. 'Where is everyone?' she rasped, her voice throaty and laden with emotion, but Ozzie was on the phone, finding out the latest on Ma'ab, checking that everyone else was safe.

Layla walked up the patio stairs, reeling. She leaned against the house wall and closed her eyes, waiting for her brother to finish his conversation, waiting for someone to tell her what to do next.

Ya Allah, *what has happened? What have I done?*

'Okay, I'm going to the hospital,' her brother said. 'Mohammed is with Ma'ab, and Baba, Mama and Khalu are on their way. Habooba is here, inside, and so are Sami and Yousif. Stay here. Stay *safe.*'

Layla swallowed and nodded.

Stay safe. Those words had never been so real.

Stepping into the house, as quietly as she could, Layla pushed her way through the curtain beads of the mini salon and saw that Habooba wasn't asleep, but sitting up in bed, making *duaa*. She paused for a moment when Layla came in, then continued supplicating. Layla watched her grandmother rocking back and forth on the bed, *sib7a* in hand, saying the words over and over again.

Subhanallah, Subhanallah, Subhanallah.

Tears rolled down Layla's cheeks. She couldn't face her grandmother right now. She couldn't face anyone.

She walked into the bathroom, running cool water over her blood-soaked hands. Layla scrubbed and scrubbed and scrubbed, the blood gurgling down the drain with her tears . . .

Layla lay in the *3angareb* next to Yousra, listening to her cousin's slow, quiet sobs. Layla reached over to try to soothe her, but Yousra jerked an arm away, out of reach. Layla tried again.

'Yasoori?' Layla whispered.

Yousra didn't reply. Layla tried again. 'I'm sorry for making us go out today, but we're all right, Ma'ab will be all right, I'm sure he will. *Allah* will take care of us.'

I have to believe Allah *will look after us.* Although she had no idea what Ma'ab's injuries were, she thought that if she said he would be okay, maybe he would be.

Yousra turned to Layla, her face crumpled with fear and exhaustion. 'No, it's not all good, Layla. And stop trying to say it will be. You don't even know where he got shot, or if he is still alive!'

'*Khair Inshallah*, ya Yousra, *khair.*' Layla was trying to hold onto anything that made sense. She needed it to make sense.

'Oh, *khalas*, Layla.' Yousra pushed herself around to face Layla. 'Fareed's cousin is in hospital tonight too because she got hurt, and there are a bunch of people missing; no one knows where they are. It's *not* all going to be all right!'

'So, what can we do, Yousra? There's gotta be something.'

'Layla, stop it! Stop it! There's nothing we can do. *Khalas!* Your mum was right. The government will always come down on us, end of story.'

Layla paused. Held her breath for ten seconds. Ya Allah, *help me.*

'No,' Layla said, drawing a line in the sand. 'No, I don't believe there is no way out.' There had to be a way to fix things, there always was. That's what being an inventor was all about. Fixing problems, right?

'What are you talking about, Layla?'

'Yousra, c'mon. We can't give up now. We can't give up on Ma'ab, we can't give up on Sudan, we can't give up! We're descendants of the Kandakaat, ya Yousra. Haven't you heard the phrase, channel the Kandaka?'

Yousra shook her head.

'It's my latest thing. What would a Kandaka do in this situation?'

Yousra scoffed.

'Layla, we're not Kandakaat. The Queens of Kush lived *thousands* of years ago.' Yousra's words were harsh, grief making her voice sound cruel. 'There's no Kush any more, Layla. We're just little girls who tried to protest in this broken country. We went out and see what happened to us? They tried to *kill* us. All of us.'

'*Allah*'s got us, Yousra.'

Yousra scoffed again. 'Layla, Ma'ab got shot right in front of us today. Where was *Allah* then? Where has he been for the last thirty years, as the country fell apart?'

Layla bowed her head. She didn't know the answers to the questions Yousra was asking. *But I have to hold onto faith, because otherwise, what else do I have?*

Layla tried to think of something constructive. She didn't know how to deal with the well of grief and anguish that was making its way up her throat. *Channel the Kandaka* . . . Layla couldn't quite run a Queendom like a Kandaka could, not yet, anyway. But she could do more than shout and sing.

'Yousra, you know that I've won awards for inventing things, right?'

Yousra shook her head at this change of topic. 'Obviously. You're obsessed with that stupid competition. It's why we had to sneak out in the first place.'

'Yeh, well, forget about the competition now.' The GDT felt so . . . small almost. Selfish, to worry about inventing things for a competition, when there were more important issues at hand.

'What if we invent something that will help Sudan? Maybe that's the way of channelling the Kandaka within?'

Yousra frowned at Layla. 'What are you talking about?'

Layla shrugged. 'I don't know, Yousra. But I feel like we have to do something. And if us little girls can't help Sudan by being out on the streets, maybe we can help by building something to make the country better? The electricity cuts out, there is rubbish everywhere and we can't even drink water out of the tap! I dunno, but maybe, maybe, we can make a difference by focusing on the things we can build a solution for.'

Yousra groaned in the darkness. '*Habiba, you* can invent something. But me? No. I'm going to pray for my brother.'

On cue, Yousra's phone started to ring. It was Mohammed.

'*Aywa?*' Yousra answered after the first ring. She listened, her older brother's voice squawking through the mobile.

'Okay, okay. *Khair Inshallah.* Okay. When are you all coming home? Okay, *tamam. Tasba7 3ala khair.*'

Yousra hung up the phone and let out a breath. 'He's in surgery. He got hit in the thigh and in the shoulder. He's bleeding a lot, but they think he will survive, *Inshallah*. He should be out of surgery in the morning, *Inshallah*.'

With that, she turned over, ending the conversation.

Layla looked up into the darkness.

He's going to make it. Alhamdulilah.

A weight had been lifted off her chest.

He's going to be okay.

Even still, if she hadn't decided to go out tonight, maybe Ma'ab wouldn't be on that hospital bed right now.

CHAPTER 21

LAYLA woke up the next morning, early. For a moment, her mind was blank, then the events of the night before roared back. A shock ran through her body, like being hit with ice-cold water, as the memories came flooding back: holding Ma'ab's body, the shots, the screams.

Shaking her head to clear her thoughts, Layla mentally scolded herself. This was *not* a productive line of thinking. It was time to get to work. The only way Layla saw she could get through this was to channel the Kandaka. Focus on what she could fix and lead the way.

There was nothing she could do to help Ma'ab now, or to change the government, that much was clear. But she could focus on what she knew how to do best. Finding a solution to a problem with an invention! That was how she got her scholarship back at MMGS, that's how she was going to make things better now. *Right?* Inventing things was the one thing she knew she could do. Her brilliant idea had come just as she was about to fall asleep last night, after she had heard that Ma'ab was going to make it, *Alhamdulilah*.

Water! To find a way to get water to the people! 'It's such a basic thing, but so important,' Layla said loudly, and Yousra stirred next to her, but didn't wake up.

Since the water from the taps in Sudan was not drinkable, everyone needed to either bring bottled water with them during the protest or find one of those communal clay urns. But . . . what if there was a machine – like a mini water delivery machine – to go through the crowd and give out water to people? Bottled water was too expensive to hand out, but maybe there could be something like *seed al-labn* for water? It could be called *seed al-moya* (the water man)! A water urn that went around and distributed water to the people. Layla beamed to herself in bed, then dozed off to sleep.

This is a pretty Kandaka move, if I don't say so myself!

The next morning after *fajr*, Layla snuck out to the shed, careful not to wake up Yousra, Habooba or the twins. She went through the junk in the gloomy and dusty room, seeing what she could find. Ma'ab's generator, she left untouched. *Inshallah he will be back for you.*

CLANK! Layla froze every time something fell off a high shelf or banged against another object loudly, but fortunately no one woke up. She surveyed the space, confident she could find everything she needed in there. *Let's get to work!*

When Yousra came looking for her a couple of hours later, Layla breathlessly shared her idea and the basics of the prototype.

'So, one thing that will help is getting water to people, right? Like clean water for people to drink while they are out protesting?'

'Right . . .' Yousra seemed unsure.

'How about a mobile water dispenser called *seed al-moya*? You might be wondering how *seed al-moya* will move about. Initially I was imagining wheels, but the roads are not so smooth, so I was thinking something like a caterpillar track –'

'A what?'

'Like, kinda like wheels with a long chain running around them, so it's more stable. Anyway! I found some chains and made it work.'

Layla stepped back from her rough-and-ready invention. There was an urn on its side, sealed at both ends and secured within a metal frame that sat on top of the wheel tracks. Layla had found a way to attach a tap to the front as well, so that people could pour water out of the urn easily.

'It's not the fanciest thing in the world, but we should give it a try,' Layla said.

Yousra was still unconvinced. 'I don't know, Layla.'

Layla cocked her head. 'You don't know? You don't know what?'

Yousra adjusted the light cream scarf she had placed on her head hurriedly. 'I don't know. I think it's a nice idea, but will it work?'

Layla beamed. 'Oh, I don't know if it will work perfectly, but that's part of the process of inventing something. We give it a go and tweak it until it works.'

'Yousra! Layla!' Habooba's voice called from inside.

'We're out the back!' Layla shouted back.

'It's breakfast time, *yallah*!'

'Okay, we're coming!' Yousra called back, and immediately turned to walk out of the shed. 'It's so hot and dusty in there,' she complained, as they shut the rickety iron shed door behind them.

'Do you think we should tell everyone what we're working on?' Layla asked Yousra, hopefully. 'It could be cool, right?'

'We? There's no "we" in this, Layla. It's your project. I am going to the hospital today to see Ma'ab. He made it through the surgery, by the way, not that you seem that interested.'

Although Yousra's voice was compassionate, Layla felt chided.

I'm trying to help Ma'ab too.

But then, if he hadn't gone to get them some water, maybe he would have been fine.

If Layla hadn't insisted they sneak out to go to the *millyoneeya*, maybe he would have been fine.

If.

If.

If . . .

An abrupt wave of emotion swept over Layla, and she slowed to a stop.

Yousra paused, then turned to see her cousin standing still, an inscrutable expression on her face.

Layla looked up at Yousra.

'Yousra, I'm sorry. I'm sorry.' The words trickled out slowly, sand through an hourglass. 'I'm sorry about, about . . .' Layla couldn't say his name, it caught in her throat. '. . . everything. I get ahead of myself sometimes, but I never wanted anyone to get hurt.' Layla's lower lip quivered. 'I don't know if this invention will make a difference, but it's all I know how to do.'

Yousra closed her eyes, her composure slipping. A tear ran down her cheek, the trail glinting in the sunshine. The cousins stood together, silent in a moment of shared grief.

Subhanallah. Yousra is a scared kid, just like me. Even if she talked and walked like a proper Sudanese woman, knew how to cook and clean and say – or not say – all the right things, they were both still two teenagers who saw their loved one gunned down in front of them. There was no handbook for how to get through this, no 'spark-notes' for a revolution.

Swallowing, Yousra opened her eyes. '*Khair Inshallah,* Layla. Now, let's go eat.'

'*Shabab,*' Layla called, as she walked into the dining room area towards the kitchen. Some of the family were eating at the table, but there were clothes out everywhere, like they were trying to win a world record for the biggest laundry day. As Layla picked her way through the room, Fadia eyed her daughter, pursed her lips and then continued to fold clothes. Her mother looked uncharacteristically haggard, presumably from spending another whole night at the hospital. The twins, still in their *jalabeeya* pyjamas, sat at the dining table and slowly drank fresh juice. Their bodies were pressed together as if they wanted to be conjoined. Since hearing the news about Ma'ab's injuries, they had been even more inseparable than usual.

'When did you get back in from the hospital?' Layla asked, but Fadia ignored her.

Ozzie, also unwashed and dishevelled, explained what was going on, his mouth full of food. 'We just got in an hour ago. Ma'ab's still at the hospital with Mohammed and *Khalu* and *Khaltu*. But,' Ozzie swallowed, and took another bite, 'the airport is opening. Mama's booked you on the first available flight back to Brisbane. You're heading home tomorrow night, with the twins and Baba.'

Layla blinked.

'What? Why aren't you or Mama coming with us?' she asked, as she pulled up a chair to the table and started digging into the food as well. *Habooba really does the best* fool. The taste of cumin mixed with sesame oil never got old.

Her grandmother fussed around her and served everyone quietly, as Ozzie continued to talk.

'Mama is staying with Habooba for as long as possible, and I'm gonna stay for the protests. It's history in the making. I can't leave now. The trolley man won't miss me. Mama thinks I should quit that job anyway. She says I shouldn't settle.'

'Why can't I stay for that too? I promise I won't sneak out again.'

At that statement, Fadia turned around, put down the clothes and walked up to her daughter.

Her long, single braid whipped back and forth with every step, an angry rattlesnake tail poised to strike. 'How can I ever trust you again, when you put your life, and the life of your cousins, in danger like that, ya Layla? Ma'ab is still in hospital, and all you can think about is yourself? Are you joking? You're going back to Australia, and that's that.'

I'm getting kicked out of the country by my own mum, wow.

Layla had never seen her mother like this before. The fury seemed just under the surface, rising up, like bubbles just before water hits boiling point. 'We gave you explicit instructions, and you completely ignored us. You directly disobeyed us. How can you make a promise like that, when there is not a single shred of evidence that you will keep it?'

Layla's bottom lip trembled.

'I'm sorry, Ma. I'm so sorry.'

'Do you understand why what you did was so wrong?'

Layla chewed her lip, then slowly nodded. 'You were trying to keep me safe, but I went out anyway, and put myself and Yousra in danger, and because of us, Ma'ab got hurt?'

'Not only did you put yourself and Yousra in danger, but you risked the lives of everyone! We had no idea where you were! When Habooba woke up in the middle of the night to find you and Yousra gone, she called me, and I had no idea what to tell her. And let's not even get started on Ma'ab.' Fadia's face twisted with emotion.

'Layla, *habiba*, you have to understand that things are different here. Before you interrupt! It doesn't mean you can't do anything, but you have to be more sensitive, more aware, you have to listen, Layla. Listen to me, now! I've been here before, and it didn't end well for one of my best friends, Ola. Listen to me. I know you want to be out on the streets, want to be a part of history, but you have to ask yourself, is that the best way for you to be a part of history? Or is there some other way you can contribute?'

Layla stared at her mum, taking it all in, then realised that Fadia had given her the perfect segue.

'Well, now that you say that, I have actually been working on something . . .'

'I don't want to hear it.' Fadia turned away from her daughter, dismissive and disappointed. 'Stop sulking and help me pack this bag.'

Layla felt like she had been beaten over the head with a *mogshaha*.

I suppose I deserve it.

'I hope Ma'ab's doing better, I kept him in my prayers this morning,' Layla offered, quietly. 'He'll be okay *Inshallah*, *mushkida?*'

'Nothing's guaranteed in Sudan,' Habooba answered. 'Now, ya Layla, eat, eat, eat.'

Layla realised that she had no appetite, despite the alluring smell of the *fool* and fresh *ma7shi* – zucchini, tomatoes and capsicums hollowed out and filled with a fragrant mix of rice and meat. As she surveyed the platter on the table and regarded her family, she figured there was no better time than the present.

'Actually, there is something I've been working on that I've been wanting to show you,' she said again.

Yousra's eyes widened, knowing where this was about to go. She gawked at Layla, shaking her head. Layla saw the warning and ignored it.

I just want to make things okay. I'm sure this is the way to do it.

CHAPTER 22

LAYLA scurried out to the back of the house to retrieve *seed al-moya*. It was loud and rickety as she pulled it into the house, a trail of dust blooming behind it. The chains, dirty and greasy, left a dark trail across the tiled floor. Yousra screwed up her nose, annoyed that she was going to have to clean that up later.

'Okay, so,' Layla stood in front of the mobile urn, obscuring the final product while she made her pitch. A bead of sweat ran down her brow.

Channel the Kandaka, Layla. Do it for Ma'ab.

'We all know Sudan is hot, right? Like, I'm hot, but Sudan is HOT-HOT, am I right?'

Layla swore she heard crickets. *Okay, jokes are not going to do it here.*

'Because Sudan is hot, we always gotta stay hydrated. We have filtered water in the house.' Layla pointed at the large blue water filter sitting on a short stool next to the fridge, a couple of communal metal cups resting on top. 'And we have water in the urns outside the house for anyone to drink from. Yes?'

The family around the table slowly nodded, unsure where this was going. Habooba leaned back and crossed her arms.

'Well, what about when we're on the go? When we're out walking the streets, maybe you stop at your local shop or find an urn nearby. Fine. But what about when we're going to a protest?'

At the mention of protest, Layla saw a wince travel around the group. She took in a deep breath and ploughed on ahead.

'May I present to you . . . *SEED AL-MOYA!*'

With a flourish, and a twirl that gave her *jala-beeya* some air, Layla stepped aside to present the mobile urn, like a magician in the final act of a trick. She then turned into a full-on salesperson. 'It's got caterpillar-like tracks so that it can travel over rough terrain, a design I perfected through my work on the GDT,' she said, pointing at the makeshift chain-and-wheel situation.

'It uses the traditional urn, but makes it *fashun*! And by *fashun*, I mean sealed at both ends and practical for mobile use!' She jumped from one side of the urn to the other, demonstrating.

'Aaaaand the pièce de résistance!' Layla wiggled her eyebrows, using a phrase for 'masterpiece' she had learned in English class at MMGS this year. 'A water tap, just like the one on our regular old home water filters, but *seamlessly* integrated into the urn's side, upgrading this classic item into a state-of-the-art Sudanese invention. The urn isn't open for bugs or dirt to get in but can be used safely by all the community. *Waaaaalah!*'

Layla threw her hands up in the air and eyed her family pointedly, encouraging applause.

Sami and Yousif were happy to oblige, despite their previous despondence. 'Ohhh, Layla. A moving water filter, that's so much fun!'

'Can I pull it around with us?'

Yousra gave a few slow claps, joining in. Habooba nodded her head, but Fadia sat still, her face inscrutable. Ozzie got out of his chair and walked towards the bathroom.

Wow, okay. That was even worse than I expected.

'So, why did you decide to make this . . . thing?' Fadia asked, her voice noncommittal. 'What gave you the idea?'

'Well.' Layla took a deep breath, her ribcage expanding, then brought her hands to her side. Her voice dropped a few octaves, from 'salesperson' to 'teenager-explaining-themselves'. 'Ma'ab was going to get us water when he was shot. If we had one of these, maybe things would be different.'

Ozzie heard this and turned around. 'You think Ma'ab got shot because he went to get water for you?' he sneered, his eyebrows knitted together into a frown. 'Far out. Layla, you know even less about this than I thought.' He turned and continued walking towards the bathroom. 'Just stay in your lane, sis.'

Layla scowled, hurt.

'Layla, *habiba*. Listen to me, listen.' Fadia pushed her chair back and got out of her seat, coming over to stand in front of Layla. The tall woman crouched down on her haunches, so she was eye level with Layla's short frame. Fadia lifted her daughter's chin so she could look Layla in the eye.

'*Habiba*, Ma'ab didn't get hurt because he went to get water for you. It is much more complicated. Fixing this country and helping Ma'ab, it isn't easy. But it's definitely not going to be fixed by a . . . sealed-up urn that you slapped together one morning in the back shed.'

Layla's lower lip trembled and she stared at the floor, her stomach dropping with her gaze.

'But you yelled at me, Mama. You make me think it *was* my fault.' Layla's voice was barely above a whisper.

'Listen, Layla. I yelled at you because I want to keep you safe. I yelled at you because you disobeyed us. We told you to say inside to keep you safe from the danger and the mess out there, and you went and put yourself in harm's way. This is not your country, Layla. You don't know how to walk these streets like Ma'ab and Mohammed.'

'This *is* my country!' Layla interrupted. 'That's why I *should* be out there.'

'This is the country you were born in, yes, ya Layla. But do you know how to navigate these streets the same way you know how to in Brisbane?' Fadia paused meaningfully, touching on a raw nerve. 'Do you know how to catch the bus, or what brands to buy, or how to even get to the shops without your cousin's help?'

Layla shook her head mournfully. 'But I can learn these things.'

'Of course you can, of course you can! But right now, you're a visitor here. You're still a guest in this place, ya Layla. So, you can't be traipsing around like you own the joint. And have you considered that maybe you could use some of this revolutionary energy for the country we actually live in? Australia? Hmm?'

Fadia caressed her daughter's smooth skin carefully.

'None of us want to see our children in hospital,' Fadia whispered. 'It's enough that Habooba was there, and now you kids?' Fadia's eyes fluttered and met Layla's again.

'Go, get rid of this mess. Then we're going to the hospital to visit Ma'ab.'

'But, Ma! I worked hard on this!'

And it's the one thing I can do!

Habooba interrupted. 'There are already mobile water filters going around, ya Layla.'

What?

'*Seed al-labn* has started taking water around on his donkeys. He told me when I saw him last. So, there is no need for new machines.' Habooba started fussing about the table again, putting more food in front of the twins.

Ozzie came back from the bathroom. 'Isn't Layla still grounded, anyway? She can't come with us to the hospital. Given her antics last night, she should be grounded for life.' Ozzie glared at Layla, his face shadowed with grief and misplaced anger. 'Just stay here, sis. We will see you later.'

CHAPTER 23

LAYLA didn't know what to do with herself. After everyone had left for the hospital, save for herself and Habooba, Layla threw herself on the couch in front of the television and let out a loud, strangled sound. 'AaaaaaaahhhhhhhhhAGGGH-HHHHHHHHH!' she yelled.

Habooba came running – or medium speed walking, but that was running for her – to find the source of the strange roar.

'Layla? Is that you?? Are you okay?' She found her granddaughter face down in the couch, braids splayed out like overturned spaghetti, punching the pillows next to her head. 'Layla, Layla, Layla, what are you doing? Sit up, sit up.'

Groaning, Layla straightened to sit next to her grandmother, wiping tears from her face. Habooba made soothing noises, rubbing Layla's back and calming her down.

'I just feel so useless, Habooba,' Layla confessed after a moment. 'Everything is so messed up. I tried to channel the Kandaka as you said, by taking the lead and doing what I wanted to do, but then at the protests Ma'ab got hurt. Then to fix it I thought I could build something that would make things better, but even you think it is rubbish. And my superpower is supposed to be inventing things. Using science and engineering and my brain to fix problems. But it didn't work! So, what am I supposed to do? Plus, I got myself grounded and Baba took my phone, and took me off the GDT team.'

'Mmm.' Habooba nodded, listening. 'I have heard a lot about this GDT team. You must really love it, if you're willing to risk so much.' Habooba paused. 'Tell me, what do you love about it?'

Layla considered it.

'It's not really about the competition, though it is nice to win,' Layla explained. 'The team is a bit tricky too, because I like doing things myself. I don't need anyone's help to invent things, and in this team, I have to work with Peter.' Layla chuckled. 'I got into a fight with him at the beginning of the year.'

'A fight?'

'Ah yeh, it's a long story. He's the chairman's son, you see,' Layla explained.

Habooba laughed knowingly. 'Always the sons of important men causing trouble.'

Layla appreciated her grandmother's understanding. 'Right? Anyway, I ended up on his team.'

'So, you want this chairman's son to win?'

'We won the national competition, and we are – or the team is – going to Germany to compete in the international GDT. And Mr Gilvarry selected me to go on this tour around the globe to meet the world's best inventors! It's the chance of a lifetime, Habooba.'

Habooba regarded her granddaughter, gently.

'And why do you want to be an amazing inventor, *ya habiba*?'

No one had ever asked her that before. Layla

wasn't really sure she knew the answer. She sat back on the couch and thought about it for a moment.

'I guess, inventors fix problems. They see something wrong with the world and they find a way to make it better. Or they make something cool out of nothing. It's fun, and useful, and I like to be fun and useful.'

'Do you have a favourite inventor?'

Ah, now that was the right question! 'Oh, there are so many. Like Marie Curie, who invented X-rays and discovered a whole new area of science; or Nancy Johnson – she invented the ice-cream maker, *hehe*; or even Fatima al-Fihri, who invented the first ever university in the world.' Layla paused for thought. 'What did you want to do when you were my age, Habooba?'

Her grandmother smiled, her wise face creasing along familiar lines. '*Habiba*, my hope was for my children to live a better life than I did. And that hope has been achieved, thanks to the grace of *Allah*, more wonderfully than I could ever have dreamt! Imagine, my own grandchildren growing up in a country like Australia? Oh, wow, such adventure. What were the chances of me dreaming something like that?'

When she put it that way, it really was pretty wild. Layla threaded her fingers together, the same fingers that had built a gummy bear actuator, done their fair share of bejewelling and, most recently, put together *seed al-moya*.

These are pretty amazing hands. Thanks, Allah.

'Now, what else did all those inventors have in common, ya?'

Layla considered, then shrugged. 'They were . . . old?' she offered, tentatively.

Habooba shook her head, bemused. 'No. They all worked with other people, were a part of a team. They didn't just wake up one day and make something and then *boom*! By magic they're an amazing inventor. No, they worked, listened and learned from people around them. They tried things, failed, they tried again.'

'How do you know that, Habooba? What are you, a secret inventor?'

Habooba laughed. 'No, my dear. It's because I know that's how all great things happen. Take our Prophet Mohammed (SAW). He was a great man, yes?'

Layla nodded dutifully.

'But did you know that he wouldn't have got anywhere if it wasn't for his wife?'

Layla looked at Habooba quizzically. 'What do you mean?'

'The Prophet married a rich woman who was much older than him, and she was his first supporter. If it wasn't for Khadijah, *Radi Allahu Anha*, Islam probably would never have made it to us. And the first Muslims, they were all his friends. They became a strong team together, the *sa7abah*. Without the team, there is nothing.'

'I don't see the connection though, ya Habooba. Do you want me to get married as a rich woman? I mean, I barely get pocket money as is.'

'No, silly,' chided Habooba. 'What I'm saying is even the Prophet Mohammed (SAW) needed to work with others. We might not think of his wife and the first Muslims as a team, but they leant on each other and worked. And now there are over 1.6 billion of us Muslims in the world!'

Layla scrunched her mouth up, thinking about her situation. She had been much more focused on putting work into the SIIT for herself, rather than the GDT.

'So, what do you think I should do?'

'Oh, I can't tell you that, *habiba*. You need to think for yourself. But use your brain, Layla.

Allah gave you a good one. Think! And listen – to the smart people around you, to your parents, to your team and to the Kandaka within. After that, *Allah* will take care of everything else.'

Habooba readied herself to get up.

'Anyway, it sounds like you've got your mind made up, Layla. *Tamam.* Just don't expect it to be easy, *ya shaaba.* Your *seed al-moya* thing might have been a failure . . .'

'Hey!'

'But, *habiba*, that's just life. You just gotta keep on. The failures teach you things, no need to be sad.'

With that, Habooba pushed herself up off the couch, groaning with every movement. '*Ya habibi*, the kitchen calls me. *Yallah*, do you want to learn how to find a –'

'No, Habooba, don't mention the word "husband"!'

Habooba laughed. 'Fine, fine. *Yallah, nabil al-abreh!*'

That night, Layla lay on the *3angareb*, listening to the breathing of her cousins and brothers around her. The conversation with Habooba had struck a chord. Being an inventor was cool and all, but it seemed like the path to becoming an inventor was going to be littered with more than a few challenges.

Oh Allah, *you've really put me through my paces these last few weeks. Please, please, please, cut me a break soon. Please?*

As she lay in bed, talking to her God, Mohammed stirred next to her, waking up briefly. He looked over at Layla and smiled, whispering a few words before falling back into a stupor.

'You did good, cuz. Thanks for helping my brother. He told me to say to you, thanks and good luck with the inventing.'

Layla looked up at the ceiling, tears streaming.

Thank you, ya Rab-bi. *Thank you.*

CHAPTER 24

STANDING in the airport line with Sami, Yousif and her dad, Layla fiddled with her phone, snapping the case on and off. Baba had *finally* given it back when they'd got to the airport, but since she didn't have data or a sim, she couldn't really text anyone just yet. And Layla wasn't exactly excited about the barrage of messages she knew she was going to receive when they landed back in Australia. How was she going to explain to everyone what happened in the couple of weeks she'd been away? It hadn't been that long, but it also felt like a lifetime. *How could she leave all this and go back to Australia?*

Layla watched her twin brothers holding hands as they all waited to board the flight.

'How are you doing, *ya shabab*?' she asked. The two boys looked at her, eyes wide. Were they going to cry? Because Layla wanted to cry too . . . she wanted to cry constantly at the moment.

'We're gonna have unlimited TV again, Layla! What are you going to watch?!'

Layla smiled. *Small joys.*

Layla was allocated the window seat next to Baba. The twins were in the seats in front of them, enjoying their unlimited television time. Layla tried to make eye contact with her father as he buckled his seatbelt, glasses slipping down the bridge of his nose, but had no luck. She didn't know what she would say to him, so perhaps it was fortunate he didn't seem too interested in talking to her either.

Why is he so angry? It still didn't make sense to Layla. So much about Baba hadn't made sense for a while. Why did he make her quit the GDT? Why did he get so angry at some things and not others? Why didn't he want to talk it through, like he usually did? All these questions would remain unanswered though, as Kareem didn't leave much space for conversation. With headphones over his ears and eyes on the news in front of him, it was clear he was not interested in any discussion.

Layla slumped in her seat forlornly, accepting her fate. That is, until the breakfast food came around.

'Here you go, sir,' the flight attendant said, handing Kareem the tray. Kareem slipped his headphones off, taking the grey tray and surveying the food. He'd been given chicken curry.

Kareem glanced over at Layla's. She had scrambled eggs. Baba loved scrambled eggs.

'Do you want to swap?' Layla said. A peace offering.

Kareem nodded, his mouth smiling wryly.

As they switched over their hot meals, Layla took the chance. 'Why aren't you talking to me, Baba?'

Kareem lowered his chin to his chest, sighing, clearly not wanting to talk about it. He rested his eyes shut for a moment, taking off his glasses and rubbing his face, then put his glasses back on, opened his eyes and replied, addressing the screen in front of him. 'You disobeyed our orders, Layla. Our very explicit and serious instructions to stay in the house, and in doing so put yourself in serious, serious danger.'

Layla kissed her teeth and huffed, her shoulders rising and falling. 'But I wouldn't have disobeyed you if you hadn't grounded me in the first place! I don't understand why you made me quit the GDT just like that, and give up the SIIT? You just did that without even asking what I wanted –'

'What you want?' Kareem interrupted his daughter. 'What you want?' Now it was his turn to kiss his teeth. 'Fadia was right. Moving to Australia was always going to make you kids this way.'

'What? What are you talking about? What way?'

'Layla, how could anything possibly be more important than family? Your grandmother might have been on her deathbed. That could have been the last time you had a chance to see her. That's your mother's mum. And you wanted to ignore all that for some competition? For some world tour, that will maybe change your life? No, Layla. Family always comes first. And if you want that tour so much, you can apply for it next year. You can find another way. But you don't get another grandmother, Layla. I didn't get to know my grandparents, you know that.' Kareem paused.

'I was so disappointed that you would even consider giving up the opportunity to go see your grandmother, spend time with your family, for some competition. I was ashamed.'

Kareem sighed, a sigh of years of buried grief and pain brought to surface. Layla was stunned into silence. She didn't think that she was selfish, but the way Baba put it . . .

'And as for going to the protest. Layla, you don't understand what it's like to lose friends and family to this government. It's not a joke. And the fact that you treated it like an adventure, and not a fight for survival, well, it tells me you still have a lot of growing to do.'

Layla swallowed. She didn't know what to say. It didn't feel like this was a discussion. As she took it all in, really felt it hit her bones, she wondered whether this is what Baba meant when he said she needed to *listen*.

'Do you know why your mother took the job in Australia?' Kareem asked, in an unexpected change of subject.

Layla shook her head, they had never really broached the topic beyond 'Brisbane needed doctors'.

'Your mother had a best friend, Ola. They had been inseparable since they were babies; Ola was like family. She was also very political. Mama was worried about her getting too involved, getting into too much trouble, but Ola believed in fighting for a better Sudan.' Kareem breathed in deeply, his face betraying a deep sadness Layla had never seen before.

'Ola was taken by the government at a protest. And when they dropped her body off, days later, on the doorsteps of her mother's house, she had been beaten up so badly that no one could recognise her. Mama was working at the hospital that day. She tried to save her, but couldn't.'

Layla's breath caught in her throat.

'Sudan broke your mother's heart, *habiba*.'

Kareem looked at his daughter.

'So please, be kind.'

Layla's heart throbbed as she thought about the pain her mother held but had never spoken of. She thanked her father for sharing the story before turning to the window, tears streaming down her face.

Landing back in Australia felt . . . strange. It was midnight again, and so Layla knew her body clock was going to be all over the shop. But, nothing had changed! Layla felt like her whole world had been turned upside down: the revolution, the GDT, Ma'ab, Habooba. But here, in Australia? The crickets were singing, the customs officer still asked the same silly questions, even the air was the same level of humid: ridiculous.

'It's all the same,' Layla murmured, as they walked out of the airport doors, smack bang into the wall of moisture that was the Brisbane summer.

'Yes, *Alhamdulilah*,' said Kareem, relief in his voice. 'Our Australia always stays the same.'

Was that a good thing? Layla wasn't sure. She thought about the long battle for justice First Nations people had been fighting for centuries. *If I care for justice in Sudan, I have to care about justice here too, right?* What did it look like to join the struggle, if she didn't have a blood connection, like she did in Sudan? There was so much to learn and figure out still.

Her phone continued to buzz with an unholy number of messages coming through, but Layla let it ring, vibrating away in her pocket.

I just need a moment.

Her mind was cloudy from jet lag, lack of sleep and the wrong outfit for the humid weather.

I just need a shower, sleep and time to think.

The next morning, Layla woke up before the kookaburras. *Damn jet lag!* She rolled over in her top bunk bed and tried to sort through her thoughts.

Focus, Layla. Focus.

Argh! It was like white noise.

Even though all she wanted to do was go back to Sudan, now that she was here, two things were high on the agenda. Number one was seeing her friends. Layla messaged Dina.

Layla
D, are you up?

Dina
Ur message woke me. Sup? Why are you up so early.

Layla
Jet lag . . .

Dina

Damn. We catching up soon?

Layla

I'd love that. It's been . . . a lot.

Dina

Miss you so much. Xxx

Later, Dina and Layla were back in the park, side by side on the swings. Ethan and Seb were playing basketball in the courts in front of them. It was just like old times, but why did it also feel so different?

The two girls both let out a sigh at the same time.

'That's such an intense few weeks, L. I'm sorry,' said Dina.

Layla shrugged. She had just got Dina up to speed.

'Intense is one word for it. I feel . . . I don't know how to feel. What about you, Dina?' asked Layla. 'What did I miss?'

'*Subhanallah*, you won't believe it, but I've had a win,' she said tentatively.

Layla beamed, doing her best to mask her exhaustion. 'Oh *Alhamdulilah* for some *good* news! Tell me.'

'They're not fully there yet, really. But me and my parents came to a compromise. If I do biology next year, I can also do legal studies, and if I get top marks in legal studies, I can study law.'

'OMG, that's massive, Dina!'

'Yeh, I just thought, Layla wouldn't accept a life she didn't want, so why should I? And I'm gonna work so hard to get that grade, *Inshallah*. I'll use Shutdown Mode if I have to.'

They both chuckled, Layla's laugh much more muted than usual. Talking about biology reminded her of hospitals, which reminded her of Sudan. Layla licked her lips and tried to refocus on the present.

'Dina in Shutdown Mode would definitely be a sight to behold,' Layla said. As she studied her best friend's face, she realised something else. 'I'm sorry I wasn't around more though, D. You've been doing a lot by yourself. I should have been there more. I promise to be better, *Inshallah*.'

Dina looked up, surprised Layla had noticed. Her foot kicked the bark that lined the playground. 'S'okay, L. I know how things were.' Dina shrugged, her top loose on her thin frame. 'But thanks. It's nice to know we will always find each other. And it is easier to face things together. I'd like that.'

'Always.' Layla smiled reassuringly.

'Are you sure you're okay?'

It was Layla's turn to shrug. 'I don't know what I am, D.'

Layla changed topic. 'What about the boys?' Seb and Ethan were playing basketball, seemingly much improved since the last time Layla had seen them.

Dina filled her in. 'Seb's pretty much the same. Ethan's moving into his mum's house, I think.'

Layla eyed her friend curiously. *Dina's got all the goss these days, ay?* Winking at her friend, she inclined her head towards the court. 'You thinking what I'm thinking?'

Dina wiggled her eyebrows and nodded.

Dina and Layla both jumped off the swings and ambushed their friends on the basketball court with a group hug. The boys squirmed slightly, then relaxed into the embrace.

'Always so mushy, you are,' Seb said to Layla, and she smiled.

Releasing their hug and stepping back, they all straightened out their respective outfits.

Dina grabbed Layla's shoulder and put her arm on Ethan's.

'Listen, yeh,' she said, more forcefully than Layla had ever seen her speak before. 'We've all been through a lot this year.' Layla wondered where this speech was headed. 'But what's the point of friends if we can't help each other out, ay?'

Ethan smiled. 'Wouldn't have been able to do it without you guys.'

Seb rolled his eyes, but nodded. 'Yup, you mushy mushrooms. Gotta stick together, ay? And no more running off without telling us what's going on, Layla. You're not a one-Muslim-band, k? At least send me snaps! Ethan's are *so* boring.'

Layla smirked. 'All right, all right. On that note, anyone got a good idea for an invention?'

I've missed this.

CHAPTER 25

'DO you know what you want to say?' Baba asked her at lunch. It was time to tackle priority number two: getting back on the Grand Designs Tourismo team.

Layla was attending the GDT meeting that afternoon to try to convince the team to take her back. Even though the GDT was not nearly as important as the Sudanese revolution, it was still important to *her*. She'd talked it through with Dina, Ethan and Seb, and although they didn't have any grand ideas, it felt so good to share the burden with others. *Who knew talking about heavy things made them lighter?!*

Layla nodded. 'I'm going to follow Habooba's advice. Channel the Kandaka!'

'Yes, ya Layla, fine. But you will need more than just your ancestors helping on this one.'

'Baba, that's not fair! I wouldn't be in this position if you hadn't *made* me quit. It's your fault I'm in this situation.'

Kareem looked at his daughter with scepticism. 'Fine, blame it on me if it's easier for you.'

'Baba, you literally told Peter on a call that I was quitting the team!'

'Yes, but only after I found out you were lying and hiding, twice. You could have handled it very differently, ya Layla. Take some responsibility.'

Layla slumped. She felt like maybe her dad *did* have a point, but it was still SUPER annoying. And now she had to grovel to Peter. *Janey Mack!*

Layla got to Mr Gilvarry's office early. She knew Peter would be there early too, he always was. It would give her a chance to make a pitch to them before everyone else turned up.

When she arrived at the workshop, the door was closed as usual. Layla knocked, and Peter answered, but when he saw her, he slammed the door right back in her face. It took every inch of her resolve not to spin on her heel and walk down the path and back to the bus stop.

She knocked again, and after a few seconds, Peter cracked open the door. He then marched up the stairs and down the hallway without so much as a hello.

Well. This is going to be fun. Allah, you really like putting me and this Cox boy in the most awkward situations, don't you? Layla wondered if *Allah* had a dry sense of humour.

Mr Gilvarry was sitting in his office, looking slightly harried. Peter took a seat and Layla tentatively hovered at the door.

'Come in, Layla, come in. Welcome back to Australia. I hear your grandmother is doing much better. Fantastic. Okay. What can I do for you?'

Layla smiled darkly. *If only Habooba's health was the main thing I was worried about.* But she couldn't really summarise trying to overthrow the government and her cousin almost dying of a gunshot wound in front of her in small talk, now could she? *Ya Allah!*

'Well, sir, I wanted to see if there is any way I could get back on the GDT team.'

Layla could see Peter fighting the urge to say something, but Gilvarry quietened him with a look. Turning his attention back to Layla, he raised his eyebrows.

'Ah okay, I see,' Gilvarry began. 'Well, you'll be pleased to know that you still have your SIIT spot. Once I put in your nomination, there was no easy way for me to change it. Only you can. But on the GDT, Layla, you know the rules. Missing three meetings in a row without prior approval is an automatic disqualification from the team. Also, didn't your dad tell the team you officially resigned? Why should we make an exception for you?'

Layla took in a deep breath. This news about the SIIT was unexpected. Should she just take the Special International Invention Tour and go? *What would a Kandaka do?* Layla thought about what her grandmother said, about how she needed to listen to others and how all amazing inventors worked as part of a team. *I can't give up on the GDT now.*

'Sir.'

Gilvarry waited as Layla readjusted in her seat. She sat up in the chair, then leaned forward.

It's time to channel the Kandaka!

'Sir, I appreciate that I missed an inexcusable number of meetings, and that my dad said I resigned. But I'm here now.'

'Rules are rules, Layla!' growled Peter, the blue of his veins popping out underneath his pale skin.

Layla snapped. 'Peter, c'mon! You're the one who made up the rules. Plus, you have no idea how hard I worked to make sure I held up my side of the bargain. We had to fly to Sudan on short notice because my grandmother was at death's door. My dad wanted me to quit the GDT then and there, but I kept working. When Dad found out he grounded me, and then when he found I was *still* working he took my phone and told you all I was quitting! Also, you have *no* idea what I've been through this last week.'

Get to the team part!

'But really, this isn't about me. The main reason you should keep me on is because I am good for the team. We all know that without me, this team would not have even made it to Germany. It was

266

my contribution to the team, with the edible gummy bear actuators, that got us over the line. We all know that. And you both know that I have worked so incredibly hard. I haven't complained about the extra work. I've worked harder than everyone else, so that's why I got the spot on the tour.' Layla took a deep breath.

Don't focus on yourself girl, focus on the team! Have you learnt nothing?

'I know that I add value to the team, and working with a group of smart and creative,' Layla glanced at Peter, 'friends and classmates is the best thing that has ever happened to me. Believe it or not, turns out I'm a better inventor when I work with other people. And I'm obsessed with the GDT. It means a lot to me, and I also think I mean a lot to the team. So, for that reason, I think you should keep me on.'

Gosh, ya Allah. *I hope I channelled the Kandaka enough!*

Gilvarry stroked his beard slowly. As he contemplated, Layla noticed three figures at the door of the office – Matt, Tyler and Penny.

'Did you all hear Layla's little speech there, folks?' Gilvarry asked.

They all nodded.

'All right then, Layla,' Gilvarry said. 'That was definitely passionate.'

Layla smiled. Inshallah *he says I can stay on!!!*

'So, your main argument is that you should stay on because you are ultimately good for the team, and the team would be better off with you on it – even though you broke the most important rule, and you've been missing for weeks.'

Oh no, when he puts it that way it doesn't sound so solid. Layla assented again, this time less enthusiastically.

'In that case, how about we test that idea? Come on inside, students.' Gilvarry motioned for the rest of the team members to wiggle their way into his cramped office.

'What do you say we put it to a vote?'

Layla glanced around at her teammates, who were all fastidiously avoiding her gaze.

'Layla, could you do us a favour and step outside for a moment?'

CHAPTER 26

LAYLA made her way to her favourite work-bench in the furthermost corner of the workshop, next to the window. She hopped up on the stool and stared out the glass pane, hands cupped together in her lap.

Ya Allah!!!

Although her face was calm, her inner voice was not. After Gilvarry's summary, she was convinced that the plan hadn't worked.

Layla's phone buzzed in her pocket. It was Dina.

Dina
How was the meeting?

Dina
Winning? Off to Germany, to see the world?

Layla
Still waiting.

Layla stuffed her phone back in her pocket, then jumped off the stool and started pacing around the room.

This was not how it was supposed to go!

Layla had been sure that talking about how she helped the team would be the way to convince Mr Gilvarry (if not Peter) that they shouldn't kick her out. But . . . Layla wasn't sure how it was going to pan out. She knew that Peter would want her off the team. Penny would probably have her back, right? Matt and Tyler, only *Allah* knew what they would do. Probably follow Peter's lead, which means that it was quite likely she was going to get kicked off the team. Layla wondered if she should have focused less on getting the SIIT place and more on helping them prepare for the international GDT.

No! Layla couldn't stand by and let this happen.

What would a Kandaka do in this situation?

They would take control, said Habooba's voice in Layla's head.

Okay, okay, okay. What was the way to fix this that would be good for the team?

Layla only had one last piece of leverage she could use.

Striding back to the door of Mr Gilvarry's office, Layla took a deep belly breath, said '*Bismillah*,' and walked in.

'Layla! We aren't ready for you yet,' said Gilvarry. 'Everyone is still casting their vote.'

Layla regarded the room and saw each of her teammates had a piece of paper in front of them.

'No, wait. Before you vote, I have one more thing I want to add,' said Layla.

The eyes of her teammates all swivelled towards her, expectantly.

Ya Allah, *I hope this works!*

'I put it to you all that I stay a member of the GDT team, but give up my spot on the Special International Invention Tour to someone else on the team.' Layla paused for effect. 'To you, Peter.'

Penny gasped. 'Layla!'

Layla breathed in deeply. 'I know, I know. It's what I worked all year for, and it's a once in a lifetime opportunity. This isn't about Peter, this is about *me*. I want to show the team that working on the GDT matters more to me than getting a spot on the Special International Invention Tour. This team means more than my own personal success. I want to take responsibility for my actions. Yes, I broke the rules, so I should pay the consequence. But, please, don't let that consequence mean that I can't do the thing I love: making awesome inventions. With all of you.'

With that, Layla turned on her heel and walked out of the room.

Layla sat back on the stool at her favourite workbench and started humming tunelessly. Just as she was getting into it, her phone buzzed again. This time, it was a call from Sudan.

Layla picked up, hoping it was news about Ma'ab.

'Allo?' she whispered, not wanting to alert her teammates that she was on the phone.

'Layla, it's me, Yousra.'

'OMG, Yousra, it's so good to hear from you. What's up?'

'I thought you might want to know that they've released Ma'ab from hospital. He's doing so much better now, *Alhamdulilah*. Do you want to talk to him?'

'Yes!'

Rustling, as the phone was passed along. Layla could hear the background noise of Khartoum, and a pang of nostalgia hit her. Sudan was so complicated, but there was still a part of her heart that lived there. It might not be home right now, but there was always home there for her. That was something.

'Layla?' The voice at the end of the phone was raspy, but warm.

'MA'AB!' Layla couldn't hold her happiness in. It was so good to hear his voice. 'How are you?!'

'Oh, much better, *Alhamdulilah*. They discharged me from the hospital, so I'm just now home and resting, *Alhamdulilah*.'

'OMG. No one would tell me anything. I was so scared. I'm so sorry, Ma'ab.' Layla was suddenly filled with shame, she was the reason he was injured, after all.

'Sorry? Layla, *askuti yallah*. What are you talking about? It's the zift government and their army cronies who need to be sorry, not you! You were just trying to get involved! Don't be silly, I'm fine. Thanks for getting me to the hospital in time too. Every minute counts, lil cousin. Miss you, *ya sa3looga*.'

Layla felt her stomach unclench and the tightness in her chest ease slightly. She hadn't realised it, but she had been holding tension in her body this whole time, worried there would be bad news on the other end of the line. Now she could relax.

'Ahh, *Alhamdulilah*! So, what else is going on over there?'

'Well, I'm stuck in the house, so I will be working on getting that generator back up. Mama is not letting me out of her sight, you know. The protests are a bit quieter now, but we're not going to stop. Haha! I heard about the *seed al-moya* disaster too.'

'Hey! It wasn't a disaster!'

Ma'ab laughed, and Layla smiled. It was so nice to hear her cousin's trademark hyena hoot echo into her ear. 'Oh but, Layla, you're not missing out on anything, the rubbish collectors *still* haven't come and the smell is starting to come into the house.'

Layla was suddenly hit with a lightning bolt of an idea, a real pièce de résistance.

'Layla, we're ready for you!' Gilvarry called.

'I've gotta go. Talk to you later, *Inshallah*. LOVE YOU!'

Layla slowly walked back into the tech teacher's office, head down. She didn't want to make eye contact with anyone, in case their facial expressions gave their betrayal away.

They're gonna throw me under the bus, I can feel it.

She stood at the entrance to Gilvarry's office.

'Well,' Mr Gilvarry started, but Peter interrupted.

'I was so pissed off at you for totally bailing on us, you know that?' Peter said.

'*Shhh!*' Penny shushed Peter. 'Let Gilvarry speak.'

Peter ignored Penny and continued speaking to Layla anyway. 'Especially since you stopped coming to meetings just after you won the spot on the international tour. I thought, oh, she's got what she wants now, she doesn't care about us any more.'

Peter got up off his seat and walked towards Layla, standing directly in front of her. 'I was so ready to kick you off the team, Layla. Really, I was.' Peter then waved in the direction of Penny, Matt and Tyler. 'It was actually these lot who convinced me otherwise. You have them to thank.'

Layla's mouth was dry. *Wait, does that mean what I think it means?*

Peter chuckled, seeing the expression on Layla's face. 'Yeh. It means you're coming to Germany for the international GDT, Layla Hussein.'

Layla let out a little squeal. 'Oh, *Alhamdulilah*!'

Gawking at Penny, Matt and Tyler, she ran over (it wasn't far, the room was *very* small) and gave them a huge group hug. All of them seemed a bit shocked and mildly uncomfortable with the level of group intimacy.

'Um, uh, thanks, L. Cool, yeh,' said Matty, awkwardly escaping from Layla's grasp.

'I don't think I provided consent for that hug, you know,' said Tyler, teasingly.

'Aw, I'm sorry!' said Layla, blushing slightly under her melanin. 'I'm just so thankful for you all. Thanks for keeping me in the team.'

'Don't be silly. We couldn't do this without you. Even Peter knows that.'

They turned to Peter, who shrugged. That was the best she was gonna get. Layla nodded in acknowledgement.

'All right, team, enough with all this. Let's get to work!' Peter announced, clapping his hands together.

'Actually, there is one more thing I'd like to say, if possible?' Layla said.

Everyone swivelled to her.

'Have you guys come up with a new idea yet for the global competition?' she asked, and they all shook their heads.

'Okay, great. So, listen. I've got an idea. A problem to fix, and it's a problem in Sudan. The only thing is, I don't have a full solution yet. And I know I usually come to meetings with a solution thought through, but maybe we can figure out how to build this thing together?'

'Are you gonna tell us what the idea is, Layla?' Peter asked warily.

Layla squeezed the tips of her fingers together, flexing. 'One of the challenges in Sudan is that the rubbish system doesn't really work like it should.

And even though people live pretty sustainably and they don't have as much rubbish as other countries, there's no regular collection, no recycling bins, no compost, you know, all the good stuff.'

Layla turned to the whiteboard next to Gilvarry's desk and picked up a marker, starting a sketch. 'I was thinking of building a little machine that can go around the streets autonomously and collect rubbish, then sort it and process it. All in one machine.'

Gilvarry's eyes opened wide. 'All in one machine? Is that even possible?'

Layla grinned as she drew. 'That's why it's an invention, Mr Gilvarry! We could use caterpillar tracks, here and then –'

Penny jumped in, picking up another marker and adding to the sketch. 'Why don't we use a vacuum to suck up rubbish, with some sort of filter?'

Layla hummed. '*Hmm*, a vacuum would just suck up all the dirt from the street, and Sudan is pretty much desert, so it would suck up the Sahara,' she chuckled, but then saw Penny's downcast face.

That's not being a team player, Layla. Remember to play as a team!

'But that is a good start,' she added, then began

circling other parts of Penny's sketch. 'Plus, the filter is a great idea, something that filters the stuff that gets picked up into different categories, like plastic, organic or metal.'

Tyler's voice piped up. 'I have been wanting to develop some faster processes for how to breakdown material so that it can be recycled. I've got some thoughts, but it's all a bit of a work in progress.'

'Work in progress is great, mate,' Peter said, businesslike. 'Do you have any of those ideas with you?'

Tyler nodded and went to get his iPad.

Matt, who was staring up at the ceiling, suddenly shouted. 'OH!'

Layla jumped. 'Sup, Matt?'

'Why don't we use those hands that didn't work from the last invention? The ones that failed and we replaced with the gummy actuators? They'd actually be pretty good for something like this, right?'

Layla looked at her teammates. Their eyes were burning with curiosity and possibility. Even Peter's.

'I think we're onto something, Matt!'

Layla sat at the bus stop later that day, waiting for her ride home. She felt sad about the fact that she was no longer going on the Special International Invention Tour, especially as she'd worked so hard. But the fact that her team were working together to build something for Sudan was *so good*. It was only a small seed of hope among the huge plain of despair, but it was enough to make Layla feel she was making a positive difference, taking the future into her own hands, truly channelling the Kandaka. *Alhamdulilah!* And after all those conversations with Ma'ab about the rubbish, this was hopefully something they could send over, something that could be useful. It might not work the first time, but it could be a prototype, and it would get the issue of rubbish in Sudan on the map.

That's gotta be something, right?

She couldn't wait to tell Dina, Ethan and Seb about the new invention. Plus she knew that her parents would be proud of her for giving up her spot on the SIIT for the team, and for a greater cause. As for trying to bring some of that revolutionary spirit to Australia, she hadn't quite figured that out yet, but she knew that zeal for justice was in her now and it wasn't going away any time soon. If she was going to claim Australia, if Australia was as much a home as Sudan was, she was gonna have to find a way to make her mark here too.

It's for you, Allah, too. I have a feeling this was one of those tests. I hope I passed!

There was just one more thing she had to do before everything was sorted for Germany.

Layla let out a little squeal as the fizz of possibility made its way up her spine.

Sure, she had more questions than answers, and wasn't totally sure that the team would pull off this new invention in time, but one thing was for certain – she didn't have to do it alone. Turns out channelling the Kandaka had its perks.

Who wouldn't want to be a Nubian Queen?

CHAPTER 27

Dear Special International Invention Tour Board,

I hope this finds you well. My name is Layla Kareem Abdel-Hafiz Hussein, and I was selected by my tech teacher, Mr Gilvarry, to be the Australian representative on the Special International Invention Tour this year. I cannot tell you how EXCITED I was when I got this news. It was all I wanted, a dream come true.

However, sometimes things don't quite go to plan. My grandma in Sudan got really sick, so my family and I had to rush back to Khartoum to see her, as my mum is the family doctor. This meant that I missed out on the GDT team meetings so I was going to be kicked off the team. Anyway, to cut a long story short, I made a deal with my teammates. I would give up my coveted spot on the SIIT, if they would let me stay on the team. They agreed.

Why am I telling you this story? Well, let me tell you one more thing. I've got a 17-year-old cousin, Ma'ab, who lives in Sudan. He's not an inventor himself, but he's a great tinkerer, and he has been our man on the ground in Sudan, helping my GDT team develop our entry into the international competition, testing it so that we know it WORKS for the people we are building it for. He also happened to get shot during the protests in Sudan a few weeks ago, so he's had a rough year. But without my cousin, we wouldn't have been able to make a machine that was not only an amazing invention, but something people in Sudan could actually use.

That's what makes our machine special. We, the Australian team, have built an incredible amphibious waste machine that is going to transform the Nile River, I'm sure of it! It's not only brilliant, it's practical and affordable, and Ma'ab helped us make that happen.

Now, making a difference for a country is amazing. But I think there's also an opportunity to make a difference for one person as well. Would you consider an extra GDT spot for Ma'ab? He's never had a chance to leave Sudan, and I can assure you he will be an incredible representative for the country. The impact it would have on him – and on the community once the project is complete – will be pretty amazing. I also want to do something nice for my cousin. He almost died fighting for freedom, and I just want to make a positive difference in his life. There's nothing like the magic of the GDT, and I want him to experience that. If you prefer I give up my spot for him, I will. There's always next year for me. This may be Ma'ab's only chance.

Yours in inventing,
Layla Hussein

GLOSSARY

3ama – aunty, dad's side

3angareb/s – Sudanese bed/s

3imma/s – Sudanese male turban/s

3isha – night prayer

3mu – uncle, on dad's side

7afla – bus

7amam – toilet

7ila – neighbourhood

7ureya, salam wa 3adala! Madaneeya khiyar alsha3b! – Freedom, peace and justice! Civilian rule is the choice of the people!

abaya/s – a type of outfit/long plain dresses

agasheh – spicy meat skewers

Ah-ha ya shabab, e7na wa9alna – All right y'all, we've arrived

Al7 – shorthand for *Alhamdulilah*

Al-Fatiha – opening verse of the Quran

Alhamdulilah – Thanks be to God (prayer)

Allah – God

Allahu a3lam – God knows

Allahu akbar, Allahu akbar – God is the greatest, God is the greatest (the first line of the call to prayer)

Almuhim ya ustazah, fi wai fai ana mumkin asta3mal? – More importantly, ma'am, is there wifi I can use?

al-mustashfa – the hospital

amshy – go on, walk

Ana min hina – I am from here

Ana Sudaniya – I am Sudanese

ara7 – c'mon

aseeda – type of Sudanese jelly bread

askuti – be quiet

asr – afternoon prayer

Astaghfirullah – I seek forgiveness from *Allah*

athan – call to prayer

aywa – yes

baba – dad

bamiya – okra

banoota – girly

barra – outside

bayd tashtoosh – specially fried eggs

bilahi – oh really

Bismillah – In the name of *Allah*

dhuhur – midday prayer

Dibita3tik? – Is this yours?

duaa – supplication

e7na hina – we're here

fajr – morning prayer

Fi wai fai? – Is there wifi?

fool – type of Sudanese dish

Gulti shinu, ya bit? – What did you say, girl?

habiba/habibi – darling/sweetie

habooba – grandma

haram – forbidden

Imam – Muslim priest/leader of Muslim community
Inshallah – if God wills
Inshallah khair/khair Inshallah – if God wills well
Inti min wayn, ya bitana? – Where are you from, our girl?
Inti Sudaniya – You are Sudanese

jalabeeya – Sudanese outfit, long flowy robe
jamel – camel
jannah – heaven
jiks – boyfriend
jum3ah – Friday congregation prayer

Kandaka/Kandakaat – Nubian Queen/s
khalas – enough
khaltu – aunty, mother's side
khalu – uncle, mother's side
khawajaat – white people/foreigners
khutbah – sermon
kisra – thin, fermented bread, like a crepe

la – no
La ba'sa tahoorun Inshallah – Do not worry, this will be a purification for you, *Allah* willing

Low sama7ti, madam – If you would please, madam

ma7shi – stuffed vegetables
mabrook – congratulations
madaneeya – civilian government
mafi mushkilla – no worries
Mashallah – appreciation for what God has willed
Mashayti wayn? – Where did you go?
masjid – mosque
Mi-jakisni – He's my boyfriend
millyoneeya – protest of millions
min thaniiiii yatil Wadaaaaa – from the valley of Wada
mogshaha – traditional Sudanese broom
mu'athin – person who is calling the *athan*
mufraka – Sudanese spatula stirrer
mulaa7 – red Sudanese stew
mumkin – maybe
mumtaz – excellent
Mush khalas? – Isn't that enough?
mushkida? – right, or isn't it?
muslaya – prayer mat

nabil al-abreh – let's soak the leaves of the *abreh* drink *nas* – people

nasheed – an Islamic poem that is sung without instruments (acapella)

qiyadah – sit-in

rak3aat – units of prayer

raksha/rakshaat – tuk tuk/s

Rasik nashif, mushkida? – You are stubborn, right?

sa7abah – the Prophet's companions

sabah alkhair – good morning

sabah alnoor – good morning (different style, technically light of the morning)

seed al-labn – milkman

seed al-moya – water keeper

shabab – youth

shibshib – thongs

shoofy – look

Shufti Ma'ab? – Have you seen Ma'ab?

shukran – thank you

sib7a – rosary beads

souq – market

Subhanallah – Glory to God

sum3a – reputation

Ta3al ya zoul – Come here, dude
Ta3ali hina, ya habiba – Come here, darling
tab3n – of course
tamam – all right, okay
tasba7 3ala khair – goodnight
toub – a piece of clothing

wa7ashteena – we miss you
wa khalas – and that's that
wallahi – I swear on *Allah*
wudhu – ablution before prayer

ya – oh
ya bit – you girl
ya3ni – kind of
yallah – c'mon
ya-nahr-abyad – oh, the white river
ya-nahr-aswad – oh, the black river
ya shabab – oh kids/oh youth

zugaga – little street

Acknowledgements

I wrote the first draft of this book at the tail end of the 2018/2019 Sudanese uprising, and finished it off as the 2020 Black Lives Matter movements were sweeping the globe, following the murder of George Floyd. As such, it would be remiss of me not to acknowledge the hundreds and thousands of organisers, activists, protestors and ordinary people who have taken it upon themselves to fight for a better world for us all. This book was inspired by your efforts and sacrifice. Thank you.

Closer to home, I am ever so deeply grateful for my agent, Clare Forster; my publisher, Holly

Toohey; and my editor, Jess Owen. Thank you for believing in me and helping shape my whiff of an idea into a real book, for giving me the space to grow as a writer, and for allowing Layla another chance to shine. For my friends, family and first readers – Al-Khawajah, Sophie Hardcastle, Beejay Silcox – thank you for your patience, your kind notes, and your gentle encouragement as I rode the waves of writerly resistance. For my Sudanese family, thank you for keeping me humble and for making sure I never forget my roots. Most of all, thank you, Allah, for the blessings I continue to enjoy in this world. *Khair Inshallah*, always.

ABOUT THE AUTHOR

Yassmin Abdel-Magied is a Sudanese-Australian writer, broadcaster and award-winning social advocate with a former life as an engineer.

Yassmin trained as a mechanical engineer and worked on oil and gas rigs for a number of years before becoming a writer and broadcaster in 2016. She published her debut memoir, *Yassmin's Story*, at age 24, and followed up with her first teen novel, *You Must Be Layla*, which she is now adapting for screen. Yassmin's critically acclaimed essays have been published in numerous anthologies globally, and her current affairs commentary can be found in *TIME*, *Guardian* and *Teen Vogue*, among others. Yassmin is also a regular on the BBC, Aljazeera, TRT and Monocle 24.

Yassmin founded Youth Without Borders at the age of 16, leading it for nine years. Since then, she co-founded two other organisations, and is now a globally sought-after advisor on issues of social justice – focused on race, gender and faith. She has travelled to 24 countries delivering keynotes on inclusive leadership, tackling unconscious bias and achieving substantive change. Yassmin's internationally acclaimed TED talk, *What does my headscarf mean to you?*, has been viewed over two million times and was chosen as one of TED's top ten ideas of 2015.

In all her work, Yassmin is an advocate for transformative justice and a fairer, safer world for all.

HAVE YOU READ

YOU MUST BE LAYLA?

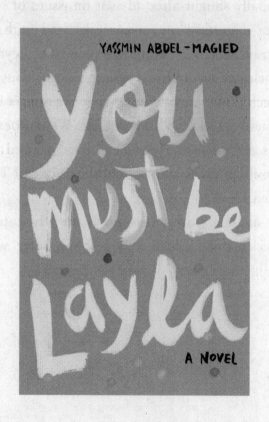